8-12

Venus
Spring

Body ★ Double

Jonny Zucker writes for children, teenagers and adults. His first novel for Piccadilly was the teen title *One Girl, Two Decks, Three Degrees of Love*, which was serialised by BBC radio. Jonny lives in North London with his wife and young children.

Venus Spring

Body ⭐ Double

JONNY ZUCKER

PICCADILLY PRESS • LONDON

For Mum and Dad

Thanks to Sarah Franzl – a brilliant stuntwoman and a great project consultant; Brenda Gardner, Ruth Williams and Melissa Patey at Piccadilly – for really getting behind this book; Janice Swanson at Curtis Brown– for keeping me on task; Susan, Hilary, Lai-Ming,Germaine, Khalid and all other staff at AP library – for their support and kindness; and above all, Fi – for her encouragement and sense of humour.

First published in Great Britain in 2006
by Piccadilly Press Ltd,
5 Castle Road, London NW1 8PR
www.piccadillypress.co.uk

Text copyright © Jonny Zucker, 2006

A catalogue record for this book is available
from the British Library

ISBN: 1 85340 873 5 (trade paperback)
ISBN-13: 978 1 85340 873 1

1 3 5 7 9 10 8 6 4 2

Printed and bound in Great Britain by Bookmarque Ltd
Cover design and text design by Simon Davis
Cover illustration by Nicola Taylor
Animation drawings by Polly Holt
Typesetting by M Rules, London

Set in 11 point Palatino and Avant Garde

WEDNESDAY

The spiky claw shot furiously towards Venus Spring's face. She parried it with her right arm and high-kicked the hideous purple beast in the centre of its grotesque, gooey chest. The beast reeled backwards a couple of paces, but managed to steady itself before lashing out again with one of its eight sharp tentacles. Venus dived past instantly and the tentacle hissed through the air, narrowly missing her head. She back-flipped to her feet and kicked the beast hard on its crusty spine. The beast howled in pain and crumpled to the floor.

'OK – STOP THERE!'

The call came from Venus's granddad, Dennis Spring. He was one of the UK's top stuntmen and was currently working as stunt co-ordinator on a big budget British/American thriller called *Fallen Beasts*. Venus was spending the last couple of days of her summer holiday on the set with him at Elstree Studios in north-west London.

An actress called Nadia Fortune was doing this battle scene with the beast in the film, but she was struggling with the fight moves. Dennis had asked Venus to step in and show Nadia how it should be done.

•• | ••

Venus relaxed, walked over to the beast and reached out her arm to help it to its feet. The beast stood, grabbed for its head and yanked it off, revealing the smiling, shaven head of Rex Lincoln – a well-known stuntman.

Dennis was working with the film's second unit, directing all of the movie's stunt scenes. He shouted at a couple of lighting technicians to get rid of some of the sun's glare and had a quick chat with Nadia.

As Nadia listened earnestly to what Dennis was saying, Venus strolled off the set and glanced up at the walkway ahead.

It was crowded with people: two men were lugging a giant barrel of plastic fish, a flustered costume-fitter was running behind the tempestuous actress Saffron Ritchie, trying to squeeze her into the tightest of corsets and some eighteenth-century Russian soldiers were swearing in a dialect that was more east London than eastern European.

Then something further down the path caught Venus's eye. In the distance, a lone female figure was marching purposefully forward. Venus stared at the long confident strides and the tightly scraped back ponytail.

There was no mistaking it. It was DCI Radcliff.

Venus swallowed nervously as prickles of anxiety flecked her skin.

What the hell is Radcliff doing here?

Venus had always looked older than her age and now, at fourteen, she could easily pass for sixteen. She had large brown eyes and flowing brown hair. People often said she looked striking, and very like her mother, Gail.

At the beginning of secondary school, Venus had started to spend large parts of each holiday on film sets with Dennis who got to work on some massive movies with plenty of British and Hollywood megastars. But Venus wasn't interested in catching glimpses of A-list actors and actresses. She was there to observe the stunt artists. At the age of eleven Venus had decided that she was going to be a stuntwoman. Venus's heroine was American stunt woman, Kelly Tanner. In Venus's book, she was the best.

When she'd first asked Dennis to teach her some stunt skills, he'd refused point blank. Stunt work was dangerous, he said, and besides, when he was on film sets he hardly had time to spare. But Venus was an incredibly determined girl. Dennis had relented and now three years later, she was highly skilled in several stunt disciplines – like pyrotechnics and high falls. Although he was just as fiery as his grand-daughter and they often ended up shouting at each other, Dennis was an excellent teacher. In spite of his tough exterior, Venus knew that Dennis was proud of her and enjoyed being her stunt instructor.

However, Venus and Dennis had always kept her stunt ambitions secret from her mother – Dennis's daughter. Knowing that Gail would be totally against such a career aspiration (she wanted Venus to follow her into law), Venus and Dennis agreed not to tell Gail about their stunt lessons. Venus felt bad about withholding this information, but she was totally intent on succeeding in the stunt world and she didn't want her ambition to be compromised by a disapproving mum. If Gail knew even a tiny bit about the electrifying stunts Venus could perform, she'd probably bolt up the house and never let her daughter outside again.

Earlier in the summer holidays, Venus had experienced an unbelievable two weeks at Dennis's stunt camp in Devon. Learning a whole range of new techniques with a bunch of other teenagers had been brilliant, but Venus had been seriously distracted by two boys on the camp.

The first, Jed, was gorgeous. Venus had *really* liked him and she was sure – unless she'd totally misread things – that he liked her. He was coming down soon to spend a weekend with her in London, and to say she was excited about this was the understatement of the century.

The second boy was called Franco and her relationship with him was not so positive; in fact they'd come to view each other as enemies. During camp, Venus had discovered Franco and his mother's involvement in a plot to poison some land in the local countryside.

Venus had needed all of her stunt skills to thwart their plan. Franco's mother had been killed and at first Venus had been convinced that she'd killed Franco too. However, when she returned home to London after camp, she'd received a postcard in his distinctive, spindly writing, bearing the message, *See you soon.* This had completely spooked her out, but she hadn't heard from him again and was now hoping that he was out of her life for ever.

The policewoman who'd taken charge of the countryside-poison plot was a Detective Chief Inspector named Carla Radcliff. It was Radcliff who was here now, at Elstree Studios, heading straight towards the set of *Fallen Beasts*.

Venus felt her stomach muscles twist.

What did Radcliff want?

Dennis had finished his talk with Nadia Fortune and was getting ready to start shooting the purple beast scene when Venus called over to him.

He turned, looked in the direction she was indicating and immediately spotted Radcliff.

'Sorry,' he shouted to the assembled cast and crew, 'I need to take a short break – we go in twenty minutes.'

As Radcliff approached, Dennis walked over to her and they embraced warmly. Venus shuffled uncomfortably. *What is it with those two?* Before the summer, Venus was sure she'd known every single one of Dennis's friends, but then Radcliff had shown up and it seemed like they'd been best mates (or possibly even more) since the Stone Age. She'd questioned Dennis about this particular 'friendship' several times, but his answers had always been on the vague side.

'Hello, Venus,' said Radcliff, stepping back from Dennis's hug.

Venus mumbled a hello. She didn't dislike Radcliff as such; she just associated her with trouble. And after her chilling run-in with Franco and his devious mother, Venus was determined to avoid any further trouble.

'Is there somewhere quiet we could talk?' Radcliff asked, looking at Dennis. 'Somewhere private?'

'Sure.' Dennis nodded. 'There's a little place just a short walk away.'

Venus stayed where she was.

'I'd like you to come too, Venus,' said Radcliff.

Venus felt her stomach-knot crank up a level.

Why does Radcliff need me? Is it connected to the stunt camp and Franco? Am I in trouble?

Venus, Dennis and DCI Radcliff walked to the end of the pathway and took a short cut past a line of trees. This led them directly to a narrow, dead-end cobbled street, named Hollywood Way in honour of the film studios next door. The only building on the road was at the very end – a white-fronted café called *Lucky Break* – a business set up specifically to provide food for those on film sets who wanted a change from the on-site catering.

The café was quiet, with only two other customers, each sitting alone.

'I'll get straight to the point,' Radcliff began after they'd sat down at a corner table and Dennis had ordered three coffees. 'I assume you both know who Tatiana Fairfleet is?'

Venus and Dennis nodded.

'She's that young American actress,' Venus replied. She'd seen Tatiana's first film, *Knock Me Down*, about a group of teenage girls who'd scaled the Berlin Wall during the cold war. Tatiana's performance had been impressive.

'She's just finished her third film,' Dennis added.

'Correct,' replied Radcliff. 'And she's landed a big role in a massive new film called *Flash Point Nine*. Tatiana's only sixteen, but she's tipped for greatness. The tabloids are already beginning to take an interest in her, but her family and the studio she works for are very protective. So far, they've kept the paparazzi off her back, but as you know, that never stops these people trying to get exclusives. She has the makings of a big story – sixteen-year-old girl as future Oscar winner – that kind of thing.'

'What's up with her?' asked Dennis.

'As her films have mainly been shot over here, she's based in the UK,' answered Radcliff. 'And in spite of her success her family have insisted she keep up with her studies. So when she's not filming, she attends a very exclusive, private girls' school in Hertfordshire called Bertram's College for Ladies.'

Venus was puzzled. *Why is Radcliff interested in Tatiana?*

'I recently received some information that troubles me,' said the DCI.

'What kind of information?' asked Venus.

'I've been tipped off that there may be a kidnap attempt on Tatiana.'

Venus whistled.

'You've got to understand,' went on Radcliff, 'that we get thousands of tip-offs like this every year. There's always lots of kidnap talk about film stars, footballers, TV personalities – those kinds of people. If we took every tip-off seriously we'd have no time for any other police work. But this one seems different.'

She paused.

'Different in what way?' prompted Venus.

Radcliff frowned. 'The problem I have is that the informant was very clear about the time period involved. He said that the kidnap has been specifically planned for *next week*.'

'But how reliable is this informant?' asked Dennis. 'Some of your other informants have been about as reliable as a flat tyre.'

There it is again – Dennis's familiarity with Radcliff's work. How does he know about her other informants? What exactly is going on between them?

The DCI smoothed back her ponytail. 'That's true, Dennis. Informants are a notoriously untrustworthy breed and I often take their info with a giant vat of salt, but something about this one made me sit up and listen. It's just a gut instinct. It might be nothing but I've decided to dedicate some resources towards it.'

Venus's mind whirled with confusion.

And your point is?

'Tatiana is an American citizen,' continued Radcliff. 'But she's living on my turf. Can you imagine what would happen if she *was* kidnapped and the US found out we'd had a tip-off? They'd go crazy and demand to know why we didn't take any action. It would be a very dark day for the police force and a disaster for UK–US relations.'

'So why don't you just tell the Americans about the tip-off?' asked Venus. 'Let them deal with it.'

Radcliff smiled. 'Let's just say the Americans can *over-react* to this sort of information and go in a bit . . . how shall I put this . . . heavy-handedly. It would be awful if a crack

CIA team stormed Bertram's College for Ladies and found nothing more than some old hockey sticks. The papers would love it, the Americans would be a laughing stock and my head would be on the block. No, I want to do this my way.'

'So what's your strategy?' asked Dennis.

Radcliff cleared her throat. 'I'm putting an officer undercover inside Bertram's for the week. He's called Dave Summers. He's a very solid, unobtrusive guy. His cover is that he's been hired for the week to help out the site manager, a bloke called . . .' Radcliff checked a slim, black notepad. '. . . Mr Foster – Stan Foster. DC Summers will be there to keep an eye on things.'

Dennis nodded thoughtfully.

'And that,' said Radcliff, 'brings me to you, Venus.'

Venus looked at the DCI in shock. 'What can *I* do?' she asked.

'As I was pondering this situation, a thought suddenly struck me,' said Radcliff. 'You bear more than a passing resemblance to Tatiana; it actually crossed my mind when I first met you, but at that point it was just a fleeting comparison. Now I'm here looking at you, I can see that you do bear a striking similarity to her. With some new clothes and make-up you could almost be her twin sister.'

Venus felt her skin tingle with unease. A couple of people had recently mentioned her likeness to Tatiana but she hadn't taken much notice.

'I'd like you to spend next week at Bertram's,' Radcliff continued, 'as a sort of insurance policy. It's their first week back – they call it Founders' Week. It's a celebration of the local people who founded the school. It's always been a tradition in Founders' Week for the girls to go on trips in the surrounding area. And that's where I need you. If anyone does try to kidnap Tatiana, they're far more likely to strike when she's *outside* the school and more exposed.'

'What, so you want me to be her bodyguard?' asked Venus.

'No,' Radcliff replied quickly, 'I do *not* want you to be her bodyguard. I want you to be her body *double*. And Venus, remember: this means *no heroics*. We can't have you endangering yourself, or Tatiana.'

Venus gazed in stunned silence at the DCI.

On one level, the prospect of becoming involved with Radcliff again felt dangerous; it smelled of further trouble. But on another level, Venus couldn't help but feel tiny pin-pricks of excitement dance through her bloodstream. Missing the first week at her own school to be a body double for an actress at a posh school could be loads of fun.

'When you're inside the four walls of Bertram's,' Radcliff went on, 'you can be yourself; wear what you want. You'll be joining Tatiana's class for the week. They're all sixteen but you can easily pass for that age, so it won't be a problem.'

'And when we go *outside* the school?' asked Venus.

'Then I want you to double for her – just in case. On the trips I want you to look like Tatiana Fairfleet. In fact, to all intents and purposes I want you to *be* her.'

'And she'll try *not* to look like herself?' asked Venus.

'Spot on. She'll dress down, you'll dress up. As you become Tatiana Fairfleet, she'll just merge into the rest of the group.'

'I'm not sure I like the sound of this,' said Dennis, who had listened to Radcliff's pitch with a very serious expression on his face. 'You've heard that next week could be kidnap week and you want to put Venus in there? It sounds too dangerous to me.'

Radcliff smiled. 'Look Dennis, it *is* only a tip-off; it'll almost certainly come to nothing. But if, God forbid, anything does kick off, and Venus is dressed up to look like Tatiana, then any potential kidnappers will go for the wrong person. Knowing what Venus is capable of, I think she could pretty much handle any situation. I can't say it's *not* a dangerous proposal, because of course there is a strong element of *potential* danger. But I think we can minimise the risk. Remember – I have DC Summers in there. He'll be on hand at all times, especially during the trips. He'll check to see if the coach is being followed and if there's the slightest hint of trouble, he'll intervene.'

Dennis took a deep breath and blew out his cheeks.

Venus mulled over all that she'd heard in the last few minutes.

'If I do it, will everyone at the school know why I'm there?' she asked.

'No,' replied Radcliff. 'I want to keep this whole thing as low key as possible. The headmistress, Mrs Finch, your form tutor, Miss Sutton and the site manager, Mr Foster – who's also in charge of security at the school –

will know, plus DC Summers and any other officers that I have to involve. As far as the rest of the teaching staff and pupils are concerned, you're at Bertram's as part of a national schools exchange programme. You're going from your inner-city comprehensive to experience a week at an independent school. People may well work out the real reason for your visit when they see you looking exactly like Tatiana for the trips, but that's not the end of the world; I just don't want to go broadcasting it.'

'Let's say I agree,' mused Venus, 'if the danger thing is minimal.'

She looked at Dennis.

He frowned.

She turned back to Radcliff. 'What would we tell my mum? There's absolutely no way she'd go for it. Letting me take the bullet for a Hollywood actress doesn't feature very high up her wish list for her only child.'

Radcliff smoothed her hair back again. 'I've given this a lot of thought and here's how I see it,' she said. 'I saw the way you and Dennis kept what happened at stunt camp from Gail and I think we can do the same here.'

Dennis grimaced.

'She would put her foot down as most mums would,' agreed Radcliff. 'But sometimes it's legitimate to keep certain things secret. If we go ahead with this, you'll use the line about the school's exchange programme and she'll never need to know.'

Venus thought of something. 'What about Tatiana?' she asked. 'What does she think about all this?'

Radcliff nodded slowly. 'She wasn't very enthusiastic about it,' the DCI explained, 'but I wouldn't let that bother you. I'm sure as soon as she meets you, she'll be more than happy to go along with the plan.'

The three of them fell silent for a minute. Venus heard someone shouting 'Hurry up!' in an aggrieved voice in the street outside.

Radcliff looked at Dennis. 'I'll give you all of the assurances you need,' she said softly. She then fixed her gaze on Venus. 'Are you up for it?'

Venus looked at Dennis. 'What do you say, Granddad? Would you let me do it?'

Dennis paused. 'If I'm satisfied that the set-up is as safe as it can possibly be, then yes.'

Venus turned to the DCI, who was watching her with eager anticipation.

'OK,' said Venus, nodding slowly. 'I'll do it.'

SATURDAY

'And this is the quad,' announced Mrs Finch, sweeping her hand through the air. The headmistress was giving Venus a guided tour of Bertram's College for Ladies. It was sunny but a cool breeze was wafting through the air and Venus was glad she had her purple fleece on.

DCI Radcliff had asked Venus to go up to Bertram's on Saturday – the day before the rest of the girls arrived. 'I want you to get a feel for the place,' Radcliff had said.

Venus had been lost in thought on the short train journey and the twenty-minute taxi ride up there. It had seemed like a bit of an adventure when she'd said yes to Radcliff, but now, having seen the palatial grounds of the school, she was starting to think it might be a really *bad* idea. Nerves were getting to her, but she wasn't worried so much about the kidnap threat as she was about the other girls. Surely Bertram's pupils existed on a different planet to her; they probably all lived in vast mansions with servants and chauffeur-driven Rolls-Royces that took them out to dine at flash restaurants and they'd have more clothes than she could fit in her entire house. She'd have *nothing* in common with them. They'd probably all hate her and she'd hate them. And there wouldn't be any boys around to provide a distraction – not that she needed a boyfriend. She had Jed now – at least, she *thought* she had.

In short, it could be seven days of pure hell.

I could just walk out of here and go back home, she thought as she studied the headmistress's face. *But then again, if I did that, I'd have to face Radcliff, and that's not a particularly inviting prospect.*

Mrs Finch had a neat grey bob, dark green eyes and thin lips. Venus reckoned she was in her early sixties. She'd been waiting on the school's drive when Venus walked through the imposing wrought-iron gates. They'd entered the main school building through the giant oak front door and the headmistress had taken her to the Great Hall – where assemblies were held – through to the Refectory and down several corridors that led off to the various subject departments. They'd then left the main building through a large blue door near the back of the school and were now crossing the quad.

The quad was a huge cobbled courtyard, overlooked on three sides by towering stone buildings, their surfaces dotted with windows.

'Those are the Acc Blocks, as in accommodation,' explained Mrs Finch pointing up at the stone buildings. 'The girls' rooms are up there. Your room is on the second floor of Acc Block 2.'

Venus looked up and then around the quad. This place was so quiet and still now; by tomorrow afternoon she knew it would be a totally different scene.

Mrs Finch strode across the cobbles and Venus hurried after her. DCI Radcliff had told her that Mrs Finch had been the headmistress at Bertram's for twenty-five years. Before that she'd been a teacher there and before that she'd been a pupil. In other words, she'd spent almost her entire life inside this place. Venus couldn't believe that someone could choose to spend so long in a *school*. It was weird.

At the far side of the quad was a raised stone circle with a wooden cover. 'That's the old well,' Mrs Finch explained, 'and that large stone to the left of it is the school's foundation stone.'

They reached the far side of the quad, above which stood a long arch. Passing under this, they found themselves on a huge, rectangular stone patio at the back of the school. Stretching out for what seemed like miles in front of them was a large expanse of beautifully tended lawn. There were rows and rows of plants and shrubs arranged in neat lines at various intersections.

'Does the school own *all* of this?' asked Venus, thinking about the narrow strip of tarmac that served as a playground at her own school.

'Yes,' replied Mrs Finch. 'We have forty acres of land. We call the grass area the Sculpted Lawns. Our site manager, Mr Foster, tends them. That log cabin you see on the right-hand side is his office.'

Venus surveyed the acres of green. She'd have no problem finding a quiet spot to do some exercises.

'Past that clump of trees on the right are our tennis

courts,' Mrs Finch continued. 'We have several girls who are county players. Do you play?'

'I have played a couple of times,' Venus replied, 'but I'm definitely not a county player!'

Mrs Finch smiled – at least, Venus *thought* it was a smile, but it might not have been. She had the sort of features that were difficult to read.

'Right,' announced the headmistress, turning round. 'I'll show you to your room.'

They walked back across the patio, under the arch and headed diagonally across the quad to an open door marked *Acc Block 2*. After climbing two flights of stairs they emerged into a corridor. Mrs Finch turned left with Venus a couple of steps behind her. The headmistress stopped outside room number 219.

'Right then,' she said. 'This is your room. I expect all of our girls to keep their rooms tidy. I'm sure that won't be a problem as your stay here is so short.'

You should see my bedroom at home, thought Venus. *I can easily mess it up in less than week.*

'Your supper will be in the Refectory at six-thirty. Do you have any questions?'

'Er . . . no,' Venus replied. 'Everything seems fine.'

'Good.'

Mrs Finch then looked at Venus keenly. 'There is one other thing,' she said. 'I understand the purpose of your visit, Venus, but regardless of this, I still expect you to behave in a manner that is fitting for a Bertram's girl. We are a very successful school – academically, socially and financially. When your tutor group goes on trips this week, I want you to appreciate that you are representing Bertram's to the outside world.'

Venus nodded. The behaviour lecture made her want to giggle, but she made sure her expression matched the seriousness of Mrs Finch's.

'I understand,' replied Venus, willing the headmistress to go so that she could get on with the vital task of exploring her room.

'Good,' replied the head with a half smile. 'I have spent the vast majority of my life here. The school's reputation is obviously of paramount importance to me.'

Venus looked back earnestly.

OK, I get the picture. Now let me check out my room.

Mrs Finch nodded a goodbye and headed off down the corridor. Venus watched her go. Mrs Finch seemed OK, but her dedication to the school was a little bit frightening.

She's spent years and years here? Come on, get a life.

What struck Venus initially about her room was its size. It was easily three, possibly four, times bigger than her room at home. It was square with large windows looking out over the quad and the science block, with its flat roof.

A long dressing table stood by the windows, and an armchair was next to the bed. A huge wardrobe rested against one wall – the sort of wardrobe that could accommodate a medium-sized family.

To Venus's delight there was an en-suite bathroom. It had a shower and a bath and gleaming chrome fittings, just like in an interior-decorating magazine. Venus grinned to herself. Things were looking up. Her best mate and next-door neighbour, sixteen-year-old Kate Fox, would be insanely jealous. They'd had a million conversations about their need for en-suites. Venus couldn't wait to tell her and brag.

Kate was a great person to have as a best friend. She was a really good laugh and Venus found her so easy and excellent to talk to and tell her innermost thoughts. She was also a computer wizard, which came in very handy – as Venus had found out during her adventures at Dennis's stunt camp. She was the one person Venus *really* trusted – who knew *everything* about Jed and Franco.

Venus flopped down into the armchair and pictured Jed's face: his pale blue eyes, his cheeky grin and light brown, spiky hair. He was eminently cute. Hanging out with him at stunt camp had been *so* good. She'd liked other boys in the past but with Jed everything felt different. She could talk to him – really talk to him. He wasn't like most of the other boys she knew. He didn't feel the need to be cool all the time and walk around with a cowboy swagger. He was confident without being arrogant. When she first met him, Venus was sure he would fancy loads of the other girls on camp, but it turned out that she was the one he really liked.

Now, as she thought of him, she felt a flutter in her chest. She was *so* looking forward to seeing him when he got back from his family holiday in Spain. She thought for the millionth time about his forthcoming visit to London.

She'd never looked forward to anything else so much.

When she next checked her watch she realised it was nearly six-thirty – time to venture down to the Refectory.

After several wrong turns (the place was so huge you needed a sat-nav system to get round it) she reached her destination. The Refectory was a vast room, with a serving hatch at one end. There were several rows of trestle tables set out with long benches beside them. A huge white and red crest with green acorns – the school emblem – hung on one wall. The place was completely deserted.

After eating her dinner of bread, cheese, pickle and an apple that had been left out for her, Venus ventured out into the quad. It was still light, and shadows stretched across the stones. She walked under the arch and stood on the patio looking out across the Sculpted Lawns. There was no denying it – this place was beautiful. Whether or not she could actually live and study here full-time, however, was a completely different matter. She'd miss her mum, Dennis and Kate.

As Venus walked back up the steps to her room, she checked her phone – nothing. She decided not to check it again for a while; Jed would be in touch soon – it wasn't his fault that he was having problems with his mobile abroad. And anyway, he'd have to be be back in England soon in time for school.

She went back into her room and lay down on the bed. It was extremely comfortable. She'd have to convince her mum to get her one like this at home. The Bertram's girls obviously lived a life of luxury.

Venus reached inside her jacket pocket for her iPod and flicked it on. As the music washed over her, she felt her wallet in her trouser pocket. She lifted it out and was about to fling it on to the bedside table, when something familiar caught her eye.

She extracted it and put the wallet down. It was a small black and white photo – a grainy picture taken over fourteen years ago. The photo showed Venus as a tiny baby, propped up on a picnic rug on a sandy French beach. Behind her were her mum and her American dad, Elliot Nevis. The scene looked like any normal, happy family holiday snap, but shortly after it was taken, Elliot left Venus and Gail. Venus had been just three months old.

She'd never seen or heard from him since. This photo was the only picture she had of him. Gail only ever mentioned Elliot's name in response to one of Venus's questions. And she'd been asking questions about him for a long time. All Venus knew was that he'd returned to the States after telling Gail that he'd realised he didn't want to be a parent. *When you have a three-month-old kid, it's surely a bit late to realise this? Isn't it?* Venus was desperate to know what else had been in his head when he decided to leave. Her mum had told her that it came as a staggering shock when he announced he was going. *So what had happened? Had the reality of day-to-day life with a baby simply overwhelmed him? Or was there something else – something I didn't know about?*

In spite of her mum's reluctance to talk about him, Venus thought a lot about her dad. What kind of man was he? What did his voice sound like? What kinds of music and films did he like? Had she inherited any qualities from him? She certainly didn't think she'd got her sense of adventure from her mum.

One day she was determined to track him down, however hard that may be and however much her mum didn't want her to. She knew how much his leaving had damaged Gail and continued to affect her to this day – she was very wary of getting close to any man. She'd had a few boyfriends over the years but none of them had been very serious. But presumably Elliot had no interest in Venus, because he could easily have got in contact and come to the UK to visit his daughter. She'd Googled him but found nothing on him. He could be dead for all she knew.

Venus gripped the photo tighter and closed her eyes. She was still thinking about him shortly after, as she fell asleep.

When Venus woke, it was dark outside. She checked her watch. She'd been asleep for nearly two hours. She stood up, stretched her arms and wandered over to the windows that looked out over the science block. She yawned and stared up into the night sky. It was lined with stars. She was about to go to the wardrobe to get out her pyjamas, when something suddenly caught her eye through the window.

At first she thought it might be some sort of cat, but when she pressed her face to the window and cupped her hands against the glass she saw immediately that it wasn't a cat or any other kind of animal.

It was a person.

It was impossible to see anything other than the silhouette, but it was definitely someone on all fours, edging their way along the school's perimeter wall.

Venus thought back to DCI Radcliff's words. The tip-off had related specifically to this week. Tatiana and the other students weren't back yet, but maybe the person out there was doing a recce, checking out the school's security setup.

All of this flashed through Venus's mind in a matter of seconds. It also crossed her mind to phone DCI Radcliff. But by the time she got hold of the DCI and explained what was going on, the person could have disappeared completely and any leads be lost.

The adrenaline kicked in and Venus's heartbeat sped up. A moment later, she'd thrown open one of the sash windows and climbed across the small gap between the Acc building and the science block on to its narrow ledge.

Venus tiptoed silently along the ledge – the intruder would be alerted by the slightest noise and they'd have time to get away. When she reached the end of the ledge, she stopped for a few seconds and hung back in the shadows provided by the walls of Acc Block 2. She now had a far better view of the figure.

It was a man. He was moving slowly along the top of the perimeter wall.

The flat roof of the science block stretched out between Venus and the man. If she could get across the roof without being seen, she'd be OK. As Venus stepped carefully on to the roof, one thought nagged at her brain. Radcliff would probably be furious with her for acting alone. She was bound to say it was an unnecessary and stupid risk to confront this man. But Venus pushed this thought from her mind and concentrated on the job in hand.

She kept low and moved quickly across the roof.

The man had stopped and was looking ahead intently, so he didn't notice her approach.

He was wearing black trousers and a black top – clothes you would wear if you didn't want to be visible, Venus thought. She could now see the side of his head. He looked quite young and concentration was etched on his face. He was totally unaware that someone else was out here with him. As Venus reached the far side of the roof, she looked out over the edge. It revealed a fifteen-metre drop.

Venus thought about her favourite stunt artist, Kelly Tanner. She pictured her helicopter jump in the blockbuster, *Point Turn*. It was perfectly executed and, according to the film's director, needed only one take. With the prowess of her heroine in mind, Venus started running alongside the edge of the roof. She had a leaping-off spot marked in her mind and she was true to it. She propelled herself forward, kicking her legs in mid-air.

The man turned round to face her with a start but he was too late. Venus's feet thudded against the top section of the perimeter wall, allowing her to grab the man's jacket and pull it as hard as she could. He let out a startled cry as they tumbled down together and crashed on to the hedge Venus had chosen to cushion their fall. Both of them rolled to lessen the impact.

Venus got up quickly and stood in a defensive stance – all of her kickboxing experience ready in her hands and feet. If this guy was part of the kidnap plan she'd need to keep him here while she raised the alarm. Even though she was confident of her abilities, she still felt a twinge of fear in her stomach. The guy could be armed and dangerous. She hadn't given this any thought before she'd acted – it was impulse that had propelled her forwards; it could be impulse that now endangered her life.

The man slowly pulled himself to his feet and Venus moved in a couple of steps. But instead of attacking her, he stood there rubbing his left elbow and shaking his head.

'Get back on the ground,' Venus commanded, 'or I'll give you a good kicking.'

The man just stared at her.

'I said, get down!' Venus repeated firmly, as she reached inside her jacket pocket for her phone.

The man took a deep breath. 'I presume you're Venus Spring,' he said, still nursing his elbow.

Excuse me? How the hell does he know my name?

'I'm DC Dave Summers,' he explained, holding out his non-wounded arm to shake her hand.

DC Summers – oh my God! The guy Radcliff's put in here under Mr Foster!

'I got here about an hour ago,' he explained.

Venus groaned inwardly. *I've just assaulted a police officer. Not a great way to start the week.*

Venus blushed and shook his hand. 'I can't believe I just did that,' she said quietly. 'I'm so sorry. Is your elbow OK?'

'Radcliff told me you could look after yourself, but that was surely outside the remit she gave you.'

'Oh,' replied Venus, her face dropping. No heroics, Radcliff had told her. DC Summers would surely go straight to Radcliff and tell her that Venus was a hotheaded thrill-seeker who was a potential liability to the overall plan of protecting Tatiana Fairfleet.

'The elbow's fine,' Summers added, 'but I'll have a whopping great bruise on it in the morning.'

'Sorry,' repeated Venus.

'It's OK,' he said, a small smile appearing on his face. 'Just don't tell any of my colleagues that I was pulled off a wall by a fourteen-year-old girl. They'd never let me live it down.'

'I promise,' Venus said earnestly, sharing his smile.

'I was just checking the security here,' explained Summers, pointing up to the wall. 'That's why I was up there. I've checked the whole site now and it's pretty secure. The older girls are allowed to come and go within reason. The main electric gates are locked at night and there are CCTV cameras throughout the campus.'

'Yeah,' agreed Venus. 'DCI Radcliff said if anything happened it was more likely to be on one of the trips.'

'Exactly,' said Summers, 'and that's why you're here.'

'I know,' mumbled Venus. 'I'm a body double – not a bodyguard.'

Summers laughed. 'I see the DCI has drilled that into you. She's a pretty tough cookie.' He paused. 'I'll tell you what,' he went on. 'If you promise not to attack me again, I won't mention this little incident to the DCI. What do you say?'

Venus laughed. 'You're on! See you tomorrow – and thanks.'

Venus headed quickly back to her room, this time avoiding the flat roof of the science block and using a door instead.

As Venus stepped back into room 219, two men were drinking expensive whisky in a posh apartment in one of the wealthier parts of west London. One was tall with a pencil-thin moustache, keen brown eyes and an L-shaped scar on his left cheek. People knew him as Harding, but that wasn't his real name. He was immersed in a novel written by a South American philosopher. The other man was a good deal smaller, with pockmarked cheeks, short spiky blond hair and a tiny snub nose. He was known to all of his associates as Smiler – because he never smiled. He was tapping away twitchily at a Game Boy, occasionally shooting nervous glances across the room to his colleague.

Both men had flown in that morning from southern Spain.

Harding and Smiler had worked together several times before. Harding was the senior partner in the unit. Smiler was nervous and had been known to panic in tough situations. Harding had an icy disposition and always managed to keep Smiler under control.

A few months back, they'd been approached by a mutual contact. The contact had set out a proposition. It was a big assignment. After a short period of negotiating, a suitable fee was agreed.

As soon as they'd landed at Heathrow airport that morning, a car had whisked them to the stylish apartment they were now in. It was on the top floor of a modern block, with breathtaking views across the city.

They'd spent the day going over the plan and waiting for the phone call. When it came, they were ready.

Harding answered his mobile with a very serious expression on his face. He listened for a minute and ended the call without saying a single word.

He turned to Smiler and nodded curtly.

'We're on,' he said.

Venus checked her watch. She desperately wanted to phone Kate but she knew Kate was out at a party and would probably have her mobile switched off.

She thought back to the incident with DC Summers. That potent cocktail of tension, fear and excitement reminded her of her battle with Franco Dane. She remembered the exact moment that she'd realised that he was her enemy and shuddered.

The postcard he'd sent her haunted her whenever she thought about it. He was out there somewhere and she had no means of knowing if or when he'd enter her life again.

She got into bed, determined to blot Franco from her mind and replace his scowling image with the far more enticing face of Jed.

SUNDAY

Venus had nearly finished her third circuit of the Sculpted Lawns. It was about a mile once round and she'd been going for twenty minutes. The sun was out, shimmering over the trees, flowers and grass and there was a slight breeze in the air; perfect running weather.

Venus was very into keeping fit – after all, if she was going to be a stuntwoman, her body would be her chief asset – but she wasn't obsessed with having a 'perfect' body or worrying too much about what she ate. She couldn't stand the pencil-thin models that graced the covers of many magazines. They didn't look natural.

She'd slept in until midday, missing breakfast but making it down for lunch. This was set out again in the Refectory, just like the night before. It was pasta with mushroom sauce and a salad – and it tasted a million times better than the fare that passed for school dinners back home.

After lunch, she did some stretches and warm-ups and then set out for her run. She was jogging at a comfortable pace as she started her final circuit of the Sculpted Lawns and was soon approaching Mr Foster's log cabin office for the fourth time. But now the door was open a crack – on the other three occasions it had been closed. She spotted a man who was presumably the site manager standing with his back to her and holding a phone to his ear. He must have been having some sort of argument because he was speaking loudly and his tone was angry.

Venus slowed to a walk as she passed.

'I've told you already that it will happen on Friday. It's all sorted. Just leave it with me.'

There was a pause.

'Yes,' he insisted. 'Friday it is.'

At this point the site manager must have sensed someone outside, because he spun round and quickly hissed 'I've got to go' into his mobile.

'Who are you?' he asked sharply, stepping out of his office. 'And what are you doing here?'

Venus stopped and stared at him. He was a small man with a wispy grey beard and narrow slate-grey eyes. His lips were turned down in a frown. He looked pretty agitated.

'I'm just running,' she replied. 'I'm Venus Spring. I was sent here by DCI Radcliff – she said she'd told you about me.'

He looked her up and down and pocketed his phone. Then he muttered something under his breath. 'All right,' he said, sounding slightly less angry. 'She did tell me about you, but that doesn't give you the right to come snooping round here.'

'I wasn't snooping,' Venus responded, feeling her cheeks flush. 'I told you – I'm just out for a run.'

'All right,' he repeated, nodding gruffly. 'Off you go then.'

He retreated back inside his office and slammed the door shut.

Nice guy, thought Venus as she started running again. *He's obviously been to charm school.*

An hour later, Venus had showered and changed into jeans and a short-sleeved white T-shirt with the word *vibe* emblazoned across it. She was up in her room and just about to turn on her iPod and relax on her bed, when she heard the noise of large vehicles approaching.

A few minutes later, the noise had grown loud enough to scare away the birds. Now it was the sounds of girls' voices – hundreds of them. The voices became louder and louder, erupting into a cacophony of sound as hundreds of Bertram's pupils spilled into the quad. Venus looked out of her window. The quad, that had been so empty yesterday, was now a riot of colour and noise. Girls of different ages were dragging suitcases over the cobbles, shrieking greetings to each other, hugging old friends and speaking as quickly as the human mouth would permit them.

Venus was a bit taken aback by their appearance. They looked pretty normal. They were wearing jeans, T-shirts, sweatshirts, trainers. She wasn't sure what she'd been expecting – diamond tiaras and ball gowns?

Some girls on the quad were standing rooted to a particular spot, others were scuttling off through doorways, presumably eager to check out their accommodation for the year. Venus thought again about how strange it must be to have this place as your *home* in term-time.

Moments later, she heard feet stampeding down the corridor outside her room, then doors were pushed, windows flung open and suitcases dumped on beds and floors.

A couple of minutes later she heard talking outside her door.

'Is 219 empty again?' she heard a voice ask.

'Only one way to find out,' replied another.

Venus watched her door handle turn, and two girls came in.

One was tall and white, wearing boot-cut jeans, a red fleece and dangly earrings. The other was petite and Asian. She was wearing black trousers and a white T-shirt with a frog logo.

'Oh, hello,' said the Asian girl, looking startled. 'We didn't think anyone was in here.'

'Yeah,' added the white girl, 'the rooms on this corridor are usually for the girls in Miss Sutton's tutor group and we hadn't been told we were getting anyone new.'

'God, listen to us,' laughed the Asian girl. 'We are so rude. I'm Jaz and this is Geri; you must be in Miss Sutton's group, yeah?'

Venus smiled. 'I'm Venus. I'm not really new . . . I mean I am, but I'm only here for a week.'

Jaz and Geri looked confused.

'A week?' asked Jaz.

'Yep, I'm on a school exchange programme, in Miss Sutton's group. I'm here to get an idea of what Bertram's is like.'

'Oh I get it,' said Geri, nodding. 'Have you swapped with someone here? Are they going to your school for the week?'

'It's not an exact swap. I think someone from another school is going to mine. It was a last minute kind of thing.'

'Well, whatever,' Jaz said with a grin, 'you're here for the week. And lucky you – you've just met the right people to hang out with. Is that an iPod I see? Are you into music?'

'Totally,' Venus said, nodding.

'Excellent,' said Jaz. 'What kind of stuff do you like?'

Venus picked her iPod up.

'Take a look,' she said, flicking it on.

Jaz took it and scrolled round. 'You've got some great stuff on here. Maybe we can listen to some of it later – I've got this brilliant docking station in my room.'

'Cool,' agreed Venus. 'So what's this place like?'

Geri and Jaz flopped down on to Venus's bed. They looked immediately comfortable.

'How does the word "dump" grab you?' asked Jaz in a deadpan voice.

The three of them burst out laughing.

'Nah,' said Geri, smiling. 'It's not that bad. Miss Sutton's cool. The girls in our group are generally OK. We mainly hang out with Daisy and Zaynab – they're really nice.'

'Oh yeah, and we have a film star here,' piped up Jaz who was still checking out Venus's iPod.

'Really?' asked Venus, feigning surprise.

'Yeah,' said Geri nonchalantly. 'She's called Tatiana Fairfleet. Have you heard of her?'

Venus shrugged her shoulders and looked blank.

'She's been in three films,' said Jaz. 'And she's just signed up for a fourth. It was in the papers last week. Some people reckon she's gonna be a megastar.'

'At least, *she* does,' chipped in Geri.

Jaz laughed. 'Tatiana's a bit of a prima donna,' she explained, 'and she keeps away from the rest of us.'

'Why?' asked Venus.

'Oh, you know,' replied Geri. 'She's used to hanging out with Hollywood hot-shots – us lot aren't even near the edge of the red carpet.'

'So what's Mrs Finch like?' asked Venus, changing the subject.

Jaz frowned. 'She can be a bit of a dragon and she's completely obsessed by time keeping. She's really strict about things like L.O. – sorry, Lights Out. If you're found up and about after ten p.m. you've had it.'

'Ten p.m.? Are you joking?' asked Venus.

Venus hadn't gone to bed at ten p.m. since she was nine. She was a night person.

'Finchy's dead serious,' replied Geri. 'She stalks the corridors. If she catches you out of your room after L.O., you're toast. It's two hours' detention.'

'Thanks for the tip,' Venus said.

'Anyway,' said Geri, 'we'll get ourselves sorted and then come and get you for supper. How does that sound?'

'Cool,' replied Venus.

As the girls bustled out, Venus smiled to herself. Following the slightly distant introduction to the school from Mrs Finch and the downright rudeness of Mr Foster, Jaz and Geri's welcome was very positive. She instantly liked them. And she was generally a good judge of character.

As Venus sat down at one of the Refectory's trestle tables with Jaz and Geri, she realised that her preconceptions about Bertram's girls had been wrong. Sure, there were bound to be haughty and self-loving pupils here, but Geri and Jaz weren't toffs or snobbish or horrible. In fact, they were a good laugh and Venus had loads in common with them. As well as music, they were both heavily into films. Daisy – a tiny Glaswegian with mad, frizzy blond hair and Zaynab – a very tall and graceful girl with dark brown eyes – joined them. They were a laugh too.

Venus suddenly felt the urge to tell them all the true reason for her visit and explain about her secret stuntgirl life on movie sets with Dennis. But she held back, as Radcliff had advised. Maybe she'd tell them later in the week when she'd got to know them better. Anyway, they were sure to realise something was up when Venus came down looking like Tatiana for the first trip and Tatiana came down looking *not* like herself.

They all wanted to know more about the schools exchange programme. Why had Venus been chosen? Could one of them go to her school for a week? Did she have to write a report about her stay at Bertram's?

Venus batted off these questions with deliberately vague answers. She felt uncomfortable lying to the girls.

'It's just one of those things,' she explained, getting into her cover story. 'It's like a lottery. There's some central body who pick a few names at random and one of them happened to be me.'

'Can I spend a week at your school?' said Jaz, grinning.

Venus pulled a face. 'Trust me,' she replied, 'you wouldn't want to.'

'Are there any fit boys there?' asked Geri.

Venus thought about this. 'Yeah . . .' she answered, 'fit for the circus.'

Jaz, Geri, Daisy and Zaynab all burst out laughing.

'OK,' said Jaz, spearing a piece of cucumber with a fork, 'I think I'll pass on that one!'

'So I'm assuming you don't have a boyfriend there?' asked Geri.

Venus shook her head and blushed very slightly.

'But there *is* someone in your love life?' continued Geri softly.

Venus took a deep breath. At least she could be honest with them about this.

'I'm sort of with a boy called Jed . . . at least, I *think* I am.'

'What do you mean?' asked Daisy.

'I met him in the summer and we got on really well, but I'm not a hundred per cent sure what's going on now.'

'When are you next seeing him?' asked Jaz.

'He's coming down to London in a few weeks – staying at his uncle's place.'

'There you go then,' said Jaz, beaming. 'Sounds like it's more on than off.'

'I hope so,' replied Venus.

'I *know* so,' said Jaz.

'What about you guys?' asked Venus.

This opened the boyfriend floodgates.

Jaz had just split up with Howie after two years.

'What about you, Geri?' asked Venus.

'Young, free and single,' said Geri, grinning and fluttering her eyelashes dramatically.

Daisy had a steady boyfriend back home in Glasgow and Zaynab had just started seeing an eighteen-year-old guy who was about to go to Birmingham University.

Venus waited for the boyfriend discussion to peter out and then switched subjects, trying to sound as casual as possible.

'Where's that actress then, you know . . . Tatiana, what-ever-her-name-is?' she asked, looking around the Refectory. She'd already checked the place once over and there'd been no sign of her.

'She probably got here early, ate and went,' replied Jaz.

'Yeah,' agreed Daisy, 'she likes to miss the common people.'

'You never quite know when she's gonna be here most of the time,' pointed out Zaynab. 'It's all to do with her filming commitments.'

'She's back tomorrow,' called a girl on the table behind them who'd tuned in to that bit of their conversation. 'I heard Finchy telling someone.'

Venus nodded appreciatively. Meeting Tatiana face to face was going to be a fascinating experience.

After supper, Daisy and Zaynab went off to set up their rooms for the year.

Venus took her iPod to Jaz's room. Jaz hooked it up to her docking station and the two of them and Geri listened to loads of tracks, chopping and changing whenever they felt like it. Venus was feeling good. No way had she expected to be hanging out with people like Jaz and Geri on her first proper night at Bertram's.

They were heatedly discussing a new rap tune, so at first they didn't hear the knock on Geri's bedroom door.

'I SAID, HELLO, GIRLS!'

They all turned round and saw Mrs Finch standing in the doorway. She had a strange expression on her face, which could have been a smile but equally could have been a frown – *Very Mona Lisa*, thought Venus.

'It's good to see you've made friends so quickly, Venus,' noted the headmistress. 'But it *is* quarter to ten and L.O. is in fifteen minutes. I suggest the three of you get ready for bed. I don't want to find any of you up after ten. You know the rules.'

'OK,' responded Jaz.

Mrs Finch went off to spread the L.O. gospel elsewhere.

'What did we tell you?' whispered Jaz. 'The woman's completely obsessed.'

'Maybe she had a really strict bedtime as a kid and now she's taking it out on all of us,' suggested Geri.

'Nice theory,' said Jaz, grinning, 'but it doesn't make

any difference to the fact that we need to break this little soirée up. I couldn't face an ear-bashing from Finchy before school's actually begun.'

'Good point,' said Geri, getting up to leave.

'OK,' announced Jaz, 'see you guys tomorrow.'

'What have we got first thing?' asked Geri.

Jaz pulled a timetable off her bedside armchair and groaned. 'Double English with Miss Sutton and then double maths with the Tank.'

Geri covered her face with her hands.

'I take it the Tank is bad?' asked Venus.

'Worse than bad,' replied Geri.

At Elstree Studios, Dennis Spring was standing at the top of a huge wooden tower, checking the electrical cable which lay sprawled across its surface. He swept his flashlight over the small junction box and twisted a couple of dials.

It had been a long day's shooting and he was tired, but nothing would stop him doing multiple safety checks on the equipment his stunt people would be using in the morning. Dennis badly needed to get the platform fight scene finished by tomorrow night.

He had wanted Kelly Tanner to stand in for Nadia Fortune in the more complex fight scenes, but Kelly had been unavailable. Instead, a stuntwoman named Carly Fisher had been hired.

Carly was a fine stuntwoman and a pretty excellent all-round athlete, but she was lazy when it came to her own safety. This was why Dennis was up on the tower, examining and pulling at loads of cables for the third time. Carly had done the incredible jump off a Spanish watch-tower in *The Kite Chaser*, but as a result of her own negligence she'd suffered a broken arm and leg. Following this sort of accident, most people usually made safety checks their number one priority, but not Carly.

When Dennis was satisfied his checks were complete, he climbed down from the ladder and headed back to the main entrance of the studio complex. A runner – a young lad in a white tracksuit and baseball cap – met him halfway there and handed him a blue envelope.

'This came for you, Mr Spring,' said the boy nervously. 'I looked for you earlier but couldn't find you.'

'Thanks,' nodded Dennis, feeling his heart plummet as he saw the postmark franked on to the front of the letter.

The runner hurried away.

Dennis shone his torch at the writing on the envelope. It was the fourth such letter he'd received in less than a month. He swore loudly and stuffed it into his jacket pocket, shaking his head and kicking a pebble along the ground.

The letter was the last thing he needed right now.

MONDAY

Venus found herself in a hot, dusty desert. Just ahead of her, she could see her dad with his back to her. Each time she scampered over the sand dunes to get closer to him, he just sprinted forward and put distance between them again.

Her dream was interrupted abruptly.

'Get up!' said Jaz, bursting into her room.

Venus pulled the duvet over her head. 'I'm not here,' she muttered, 'try further down the corridor.'

'I mean it,' said Jaz, laughing. 'We've got to get down for breakfast.'

'I'll be down in half an hour,' called Venus from beneath the duvet.

Jaz yanked the duvet off. 'No way!' she cried. 'You've got to get down there as soon as you can – by eight-twenty, they take your food away! Literally. Geri was once halfway through a Weetabix when her bowl was snatched away. We warned you about Finchy and time keeping. It's not just L.O. The clock rules that woman's life. Plus we've got double English at eight-forty-five. If you're late for class, even by a minute or two, Finchy goes crazy.'

'You can't be serious?' Venus asked.

'I am,' Jaz replied. 'Now come on.'

'OK,' sighed Venus, 'I'll be down in ten minutes.'

She reluctantly climbed out of bed and headed for the shower. Ten minutes later, she entered the Refectory. She ate with Jaz and Geri, while they regaled her with Tatiana Fairfleet stories.

'Do you remember when she borrowed your shampoo, used all of it and then screamed at you when her hair came out a bit red?' asked Jaz, laughing.

Geri nodded. 'And that was her on a good day,' she said.

They finished their cereal at eight-nineteen and, sure enough, a minute later the three women who ran the kitchens started collecting all of the bowls and plates off the tables – including the ones still being used.

Twenty-five minutes later, Venus, Jaz and Geri entered a long rectangular classroom. There were twelve other girls already in there. Daisy and Zaynab were sitting in the middle row. They both gave Venus a wave.

Venus took a seat in the back row next to Jaz. A few seconds later, a young, tall woman, with long brown hair and wafer-thin glasses entered the room. She was wearing a smart royal blue two-piece suit.

'Good morning, girls,' she announced. 'As most of you know, I'm Miss Sutton. I'm going to be your form tutor for the year.'

The teacher looked around her class. Her gaze fixed for a few seconds on an empty chair, then turned to Venus.

'You must be Venus Spring,' she said with a welcoming

smile. 'If you haven't met Venus yet, she will be spending a week with us as part of a schools exchange programme. I want to ensure that she has an excellent experience here. It's lovely to have you, Venus.'

'Thanks,' said Venus.

'Right,' said Miss Sutton, 'let's get started straight away. The first book we're doing this year is Shakespeare's *Othello* and I'd like to begin by looking at the context in which the play takes place.'

As Miss Sutton talked to the class, it suddenly hit Venus that this wasn't just a week-long chill-out session. This was a *school*. There were *lessons* here. She groaned inwardly. That holiday feeling she'd experienced – on Saturday and especially yesterday when she'd hung out with Jaz and Geri – abruptly evaporated.

To Venus, school was generally OK. She was good at English, Spanish and PE. She wasn't a big fan of science or geography, but she got by. Overall, her work was fine. But she'd rather not be at school. It got in the way of learning to be a stuntgirl.

Miss Sutton was clearly passionate about her subject, but Venus quickly found her mind wandering. She was only going to be here for a week – it wouldn't matter if she didn't listen to every word every teacher said. She started thinking about the première of *Airborne Sword* – the forthcoming autumn blockbuster. Dennis had worked on it and the movie had already opened in the States to rave reviews. The British première was going to be at the Empire, Leicester Square. Dennis had promised he'd get them both tickets, but the event was fast approaching and as yet, he hadn't delivered. Kelly Tanner had been the lead stuntwoman on the film and Dennis said that Kelly might come over for the première. This would give Venus a chance to meet her all-time heroine. *Dennis better come up with those tickets*, she thought, before she tried to tune back in to what Miss Sutton was saying.

During morning break, Venus stood with Jaz and Geri on the quad. Daisy and Zaynab came up to say hello, but they had to go to a meeting in the Great Hall about this year's netball league.

Everywhere in the quad there was noise and colour. Some of the younger girls were running around after each other; the older ones stood in groups chatting.

'Hey,' said Jaz suddenly. 'That's her.'

Venus followed Jaz's outstretched finger.

It was Tatiana Fairfleet. She was walking across the quad towards Acc Block 3, dragging a metal case on wheels behind her.

'I'm off to the loo,' Venus announced.

'See you in a bit,' said Jaz.

Venus hurried across the quad in the direction of Acc Block 3. As soon as she was through the door, she upped her pace. She caught up with Tatiana as the actress was stepping out on to the second floor.

'Tatiana,' called Venus.

Tatiana turned round and looked at Venus with uncertainty. 'Who are you?' she asked.

Venus studied her face carefully.

DCI Radcliff was right; there was a definite likeness between them. And away from the glitz, glamour and greasepaint of Hollywood, Tatiana looked much plainer than she did on the big screen. With some make-up and the right clothes, Venus would make a pretty good body double.

'I'm Venus Spring. DCI Radcliff asked me to come here to be your body double for this week's trips.'

Tatiana raised her eyes to the heavens. 'I can't believe she actually *sent someone*,' she muttered.

'Sorry?' asked Venus.

'Look,' said the actress through pursed lips. 'No offence, but I told that Radcliff woman that I didn't want a body double.'

'But what about the kidnap tip-off?' asked Venus. 'There's specific intelligence about an attempt this week and —'

'Yeah, yeah,' said Tatiana impatiently, looking down at her luggage. 'There are loads of weirdos out there. Everyone in the acting community has some sort of creep on their case – it's part of the territory. And anyway, there's some cop guy here for the week to keep an eye on things. That's enough. Why the hell she had to ask you to come as well, I'll never know. It's not even as if you look anything like me.'

And with that Tatiana walked off.

That went well, Venus thought to herself grimly, as she headed back towards the quad.

'Hi, Venus.'

Venus's heart did a wild piece of street dancing.

It was Jed.

After morning break, she'd had maths with the fearsome Mrs 'Tank' Tancred, who shouted a lot and broke several pieces of chalk in her desire to write things down on the blackboard. After lunch, she had D and T; the lesson was about making chairs. Venus worked with Jaz and Geri. Tatiana finally joined the group for this lesson, but she chose to work on her own, as far away from the others as possible.

It was now fifteen minutes before supper. Jed's timing couldn't have been better.

Try and keep cool.

'Hey, Jed. How's it going?'

Venus felt that tingle of exhilaration down her spine.

'Everything's cool. We came back from Spain a couple of days early.'

Excellent! No more mobile phone problems.

They chatted for a bit about his holiday, then after a short silence, Jed's voice turned serious. 'I've got to tell you something.'

Venus's heart missed a beat.

Please don't tell me you've started going out with someone else. Please don't say you met a beautiful Spanish girl and that you're going to live in Barcelona.

'It's about my weekend down in London.'

You mean the one I'm hysterically excited about?

'The thing is,' he continued, 'my Australian aunt and uncle have just decided to come to England. They're arriving that weekend.'

'And?'

'And . . . I've tried to get out of it, but my mum says no way. She reckons as we only see them once every three years it would be totally outrageous of me not to be here. I told her ages ago about me going to London and staying at my uncle's place, but she isn't having it. I'm really sorry, but that weekend is off.'

OK – hideously disappointing news, but at least no other girl-friend on the scene – if he's telling the truth.

'So you won't be able to make it at all?'

'I'm sorry,' Jed replied. 'I'll arrange another time – I promise.'

They chatted on and Venus tried hard to mask her disappointment. Whatever happened, he was so easy to talk to. They only stopped because Venus had to go to supper.

At supper though, Venus was really fed up. Was his story true? If it was, she supposed it was an acceptable excuse. But if he'd really wanted to see her, wouldn't he have found a way? And although he said he'd rearrange the weekend he hadn't actually fixed a date.

She and her new friends analysed the conversation in minuscule detail and she phoned Kate straight after supper. After offloading all of her angst, she felt a bit better.

Later that night, in a central London back street, Harding and Smiler were studying the back of an enormous mirrored building. Both men were wearing dark clothing. They watched in silence for several minutes as a guard inside went about his duties.

Harding waved his hands twice and Smiler scurried

nervously across the road. He drew a tiny, silver digital camera from his pocket and quickly took a series of photos of the large glass door. Then, checking both ways up the street, he lay down on the pavement and took an extra set of pictures of the metal rim at the bottom of the door. Following this, he produced a tiny, black frame from his bag and quickly extended it into a ladder.

Smiler looked back at Harding, who gave him the thumbs-up. Smiler scaled the ladder in an instant and took some close-ups of the metal rim at the top of the door. He quickly flicked through the photos and nodded with satisfaction. At that second a police siren blared on the main road, cutting through the night's silence like a well-aimed punch.

Smiler froze at the top of the ladder. Harding stepped back into the doorway of another building. The siren got louder and the men eyed each other. Harding's expression was steely and unfazed. Smiler's mouth twitched anxiously. But the siren started to fade as the car drove past.

Harding indicated for Smiler to get on with what he'd been doing. Smiler obeyed this command and finished his inspection. In a few seconds, he was back on the street, folding up his ladder and crossing the road.

'Everything OK?' demanded Harding.

Smiler nodded.

'Excellent,' said Harding. 'Let's move out.'

The two men slunk off into the night. Before they reached the corner of the street, it was impossible to separate them from their shadows.

TUESDAY

Venus stood in front of the full-length mirror on the door of her wardrobe.

Today was a trip day. She didn't have a clue where Miss Sutton's group were going, but that didn't matter.

In spite of the abrasive response she'd received from Tatiana yesterday, she wasn't going to be swayed from carrying out the job. She'd (maybe foolishly) accepted it, and she was going to see it through.

She needed to look as much like Tatiana Fairfleet as possible. That's why she was here. That's what she was going to do.

Tatiana's hostility had really shocked her. It wasn't as if Venus was some sort of starry-eyed film groupie, pestering her for a photo or an autograph. She was here to make Tatiana as safe as possible in light of an informant's specific information. Maybe she'd just caught Tatiana at a bad time; hopefully this morning she'd be more chilled out and would see things differently.

Venus had studied what the actress had been wearing the day before. She'd been in jeans, a long-sleeved white T-shirt, trainers and her trademark Versace sunglasses. This was quite regular gear for her; Venus knew that because Radcliff had given her some glossy celebrity magazines to study. And Venus had been supplied with similar clothes and Versace sunglasses – there were some advantages to the job after all!

She laid out an almost identical set of clothes on the bed. She got out her make-up bag and looked at herself in the mirror again.

Venus didn't normally bother with make-up, apart from the odd dab of lip-gloss. When she went to a party, she'd use a bit more, but on a day-to-day basis she couldn't be bothered with the hassle. Surely, Venus reasoned, the primary point of make-up was to attract the opposite sex – 'war paint' her mum called it. But she'd managed to attract boys without wearing gallons of the stuff – look at Jed.

She brushed some blusher on her cheeks, applied a lick of mascara and a smear of lipstick. She tied her hair back, donned a blue New York Yankees baseball cap and the Versace sunglasses.

She then pulled her best arrogant film starlet pose for the benefit of the mirror.

Not bad, she conceded to herself. *Today, Venus Spring, you are Tatiana Fairfleet.*

She took one last look at herself and headed for the door.

A few raised eyebrows greeted her arrival in the Refectory.

'Hey, Venus!' shouted Jaz with wide eyes, as she poured some milk on her cornflakes. 'What is this – Tatiana Fairfleet Day?'

'Nah,' replied Venus quickly. 'It's Venus Spring Day. I had this look first and I'm not going to change it.'

'Wow!' breathed Geri, arriving at the table with a bowl of fruit salad. 'You *do* look like her.'

'*She* looks like *me*, you mean,' said Venus, smiling.

Geri and Jaz looked at each other and laughed.

Daisy, Zaynab and a few other girls stared at her with interest for a few seconds but their attention was soon distracted by breakfast conversation.

Venus was pleased. She'd obviously got the Tatiana look down to a T.

As Venus was starting on a piece of toast, Tatiana Fairfleet walked into the Refectory.

Venus's heart sank as if it had just been wrapped in a lead blanket. Tatiana had made no effort – *absolutely* no effort – to look any different to how she normally did. In fact, she was wearing almost identical clothes to the ones she'd been wearing yesterday. Venus felt pinpricks of anger flickering across her body. Tatiana's hair was tied back and she sported the exact same cap and sunglasses as Venus. The girls looked almost identical – the only difference being that Tatiana's T-shirt was green, not blue.

'There you go,' said Geri, with a laugh. 'It's your twin sister, Venus. Are you sure the two of you didn't plan this together?'

'No,' replied Venus through gritted teeth.

How could Tatiana be so damn stupid? I'm putting myself out for her and all she can do is throw it right back in my face.

After breakfast Miss Sutton's group headed for the first

of four coaches that were parked on the school's carriage drive. Three other groups were going off on separate trips.

Venus sat at the back with Jaz and Geri.

Tatiana was the last girl to get on with DC Summers right behind her.

'Who's that?' whispered Jaz, nudging Geri and Venus. 'He's a bit of all right!'

'Quiet, girls,' announced Miss Sutton suddenly, standing up at the front. 'This is Mr Summers. He's working with Mr Foster for a while on the maintenance of the site. He'll be coming on the trip with us today.'

'Hello*oooo*,' purred Geri, in her best seventies-sitcom lecherous voice.

Summers gave the group a little wave. His eyes rested on Venus for a second but then he looked back at Miss Sutton.

'The journey will take about thirty-five minutes,' Miss Sutton explained.

'Where are we going?' someone called out.

'You'll see when we get there,' Miss Sutton replied. A second later she leaned over to the driver and said something quietly to him.

Venus watched everything very closely. It seemed that Radcliff's plan about keeping trip destinations secret was working. Miss Sutton had clearly only just shared this secret with the driver, because he nodded, then turned on the coach's engine and started moving off.

About half an hour later, the coach pulled up in a car park darkened by the shadow of a huge castle.

'Right,' announced Miss Sutton, standing again. 'This is Repton Castle. Let's leave the coach in an orderly fashion. And remember – mobile phones off. It would be highly embarrassing for all of us if one rang during our visit.'

The girls filed off the coach and headed towards the wide drawbridge. They walked over the moat and under the risen portcullis. About twenty metres in, they found themselves in a big open courtyard. Surrounding them were four ancient stone walls, each one peppered with arrow slits.

'OK,' Miss Sutton said. 'We're going to the armoury first; this way, girls.'

Venus saw Tatiana taking her place near the front of the group. DC Summers was a few paces behind her, trying to look inconspicuous.

It was after they came out of the armoury, and were crossing the main courtyard that Venus heard a sharp knocking sound behind her. She spun round. For a fraction of a second she saw a boy in a hoodie. He was in her sight for such a short time that he was nothing more than a blur really. As soon as she spotted him, he hurried out of sight – through the back door of the castle kitchen.

But the sight of him made Venus shiver with fear.

She hadn't seen his face but there was something about his walk that looked very familiar; *too* familiar. He loped in exactly the same way as the boy she'd literally crossed swords with at stunt camp – Franco. And he was the same height as Franco, too.

Venus stood frozen to the spot. Was it him? Could he

possibly have tracked her down and was now stalking her? Or was it simply a trick of the light, an anxious mirage in her head? Whatever it was, she felt completely spooked. She wandered back a few steps but there was no sign of him.

'Hey, Venus, over here!'

It was Jaz beckoning to her.

'Are you OK?' asked Jaz, snapping Venus back into the present. 'You look like you've just seen a medieval ghost.'

'It's nothing,' Venus replied, smiling quickly.

There was no way she could explain the whole Franco thing to Jaz and Geri. And even if she did, when she said she thought he might be stalking her, they'd probably think she was crazy.

She followed the rest of the group, who were being led by Miss Sutton towards the servants' quarters. These were tiny and looked particularly uncomfortable.

'How pleased are you that you never had to work here?' said Geri with a grin.

'I can think of better places to work.' Jaz laughed. 'What about you, Venus?'

'What?'

'You know, servants' living conditions?'

'Oh yeah, apalling,' Venus agreed. She hadn't been concentrating properly on the conversation. Her mind was littered with thoughts about the boy in the hoodie. Would Franco really have made such an effort to follow her? And anyway, how could he know she was going to be here? She hadn't even known today's destination herself.

This last thought reassured her somewhat. There was absolutely no way he could have known about this trip. Therefore it couldn't have been him.

It was OK.

As the group moved up on to the castle ramparts, Venus enjoyed the spectacular views and breathed in the fresh air, trying to clear her head.

'Gather round,' said Miss Sutton a few moments later, 'I want to show you some other sites of local interest.'

Everyone shuffled forward. Miss Sutton was just indicating an old flourmill that had supplied the castle when Venus's blood turned to ice.

There he was again. The boy in the hoodie. He was on the walkway directly opposite the group.

Again, Venus couldn't see his face, but she felt fear snaking up inside her. The stance, the height, the shape – each one of these led to the same sinister conclusion: Franco.

Right, thought Venus, as her whole body tensed. *If he wants to play games, I'm going to take him on. I'm not going to let him intimidate me. I'm going to face him.*

But in the seconds she was thinking this the boy turned to his right and started moving towards the ruined doorway nearest him.

Venus brushed past Jaz and ran.

'Hey, Venus, what are you —?' asked Jaz.

'Venus, where are you going?' called Miss Sutton sternly. 'Come back!'

But Venus's mind could only focus on one thing, and he'd just disappeared through the doorway.

She sprinted across the ramparts and flew through the doorway after him. She could hear his feet clattering down the spiral stone steps in front of her.

Down she lunged, taking three steps at a time. She caught a glimpse of the back of his head. But he upped his pace and disappeared from view again.

Venus careered past the first floor and carried on down to the bottom. As she pounded the steps one thought kept on shouting at her: *It has to be him; it has to be Franco – the boy who would have killed me a few weeks back if he'd got his way.*

As she emerged into the courtyard she had a clear sight of him. He was about twenty metres ahead of her, and hurrying towards the back door of the castle kitchen. She remembered the layout – after he got through the kitchen it was straight back into the banqueting hall. If she could pick up speed now she was sure she could catch up with him.

She kicked her heels and ran feverishly after him. He fled through the kitchen door. She was gaining on him. She had no idea what she was going to do when she caught up with him, but this didn't deter her.

Inside the kitchen she crashed immediately into the side of a very large man wearing a baseball cap and a luminous green tracksuit.

'Hey, kid, what are you doing?' demanded the man in an American drawl. He was part of a large group of tourists who were making their way slowly through the medieval kitchen.

Venus dived to her left. She could see the hoodie boy weaving in and out between enthusiastic Americans.

'This place is so authentic!' one of them cried. 'Look at those cute little dishes.'

'Excuse me!' Venus pleaded loudly, but the Americans didn't take any notice of her. They were too busy cooing over the quaint kitchen scene. The hoodie boy was bobbing up and down, getting away. Desperately, Venus looked for options. Her eye hit upon the long trestle table in the middle of the room, set with model ingredients, platters and goblets. Without thinking it through, Venus leaped to her left, bounced off the back of a chair and landed on the table.

'What is that kid doing?' yelled another American voice.

From up on the table, Venus had a much better view. The boy was struggling to make speedy progress as he tried to negotiate his way round the tour party and get into the banqueting hall.

I've got him, thought Venus.

She was vaguely aware of a gruff voice shouting 'STOP!' somewhere behind her but she assumed it was one of the Americans.

She took off along the table to the utter shock of the tourists who were pointing at her and staring with open mouths. She was closing in on hoodie boy fast. Her feet kicked a couple of goblets off the table and made a model of a young female servant wobble.

The boy had got past the last of the Americans, but Venus was nearly upon him.

Seeing a long oak beam suspended from the ceiling, she jumped forward and gripped it tightly. Swinging herself forward, she plummeted down towards the boy. In the second before she landed, she could hear his rasping breath.

Venus hit the ground running, but the boy stepped to the side, evaded her grasp and fled to the other kitchen door.

She heard the voice again behind her, yelling 'Stop!' but it meant nothing to her.

The boy now had only five metres on her. He hurtled through the door and slammed it shut behind him. Next was the banqueting hall. She'd certainly get him in there.

She kicked open the door and lunged out into the hall.

The boy was only a few paces ahead of her. She sprinted and leaped forward headfirst. Wrapping her arms tightly round his ankles, she brought him clattering to the ground in rugby-tackle style.

'Hold him!' cried the voice behind her.

But she didn't look round. It was time to unmask Franco and face him. He was stalking her. It wasn't just freaky, it was illegal and she could get Radcliff to lock him up for this. She'd hold him until DC Summers arrived; she'd do anything other than let him out of her sight and spook her so badly again.

She reached forward, grabbed the edge of his hoodie and yanked it back, twisting his head round to face her in the same movement.

A sharp spear of shock pierced her body.

It wasn't Franco.

It was a boy of about thirteen, with a slim, spotty face, greasy black hair and a matching scowl. He looked nothing like Franco.

'Get off me!' he roared.

'Well done!' cried the voice behind her. 'Keep him there.'

Venus turned round. It was one of the castle security guards. He was bulky and had short, bleached hair and a tattoo of a snake on his left arm. He looked breathless and was almost blue in the face.

'You got him!' the guard panted. 'Excellent work! You must have seen him graffiti that statue too!'

Venus's head was cloudy. She'd been so sure it was Franco. Was she so traumatised by her experiences with him that summer that she was hallucinating?

The security guard reached out and yanked the boy to his feet. 'You're coming with me, son,' snarled the guard. 'I've already radioed my colleague to notify the police.'

The boy groaned and sneered at Venus before the guard led him away. They crossed the hall and in a few seconds were gone.

Venus stayed on the ground, and it was only then that she realised she was shaking. She was totally creeped out by the whole incident.

She cursed Franco for getting so deeply into her psyche and making her see shadows where none existed.

'Venus! Why did you run off like that? Is it something to do with Tatiana?' Miss Sutton was striding over to her.

Venus stood up and winced. How could she explain this without seeming mad?

'No,' replied Venus, catching her breath. 'It's nothing to do with her. I just thought I saw . . . someone I knew.'

'Someone you knew?' repeated Miss Sutton, a small measure of the fear disappearing from her voice. 'Who was it? And why did you have to run after them like an Olympic sprinter? Couldn't you have just called out their name?'

'It was . . . It was someone from my past,' Venus replied quietly. 'Someone . . . bad.'

'Oh,' said Miss Sutton, looking at Venus with concern. 'Did you catch him?'

Venus nodded.

'Well, what did you say to him?'

Venus was silent for a few seconds. 'It wasn't the boy I thought it was. It was someone who graffitied a statue. One of the security guards has taken him away.'

'OK,' said Miss Sutton, looking a little confused. 'Well . . . well done.'

Venus shrugged her shoulders.

'Look, Venus, you're obviously shaken up by this. Is there anything I can do to help?'

Venus stared at Miss Sutton's face and swallowed several times. 'No. It's OK.'

Miss Sutton looked at Venus, worried. 'Well, it doesn't sound OK to me. I can see you're upset. I propose we try and forget about this boy and join the rest of the group. They're waiting in the courtyard.'

'STOP!' yelled Dennis Spring.

Stuntman Rex Lincoln slammed on the brakes of the sleek black van and stuck his head out of the window.

'What?' he shouted, shielding his eyes from the late

afternoon sun. He was about to drive the van off a bridge and into a pool of water.

'You're off the mark,' Dennis shouted. He'd had a long white line painted out of shot to keep the van inside a safe perimeter.

'No way!' Rex protested, looking at the ground. 'I'm easily in the zone. What's your problem?'

'It's not *my* problem!' exclaimed Dennis, striding over to the van and indicating that one of the van's wheels was halfway over the line.

'Come on, Dennis,' pleaded Rex. 'We're talking *millimetres* here.'

Dennis shook his head. 'Millimetres separate life and death, Rex. You know that. Reverse and get back into the starting circle.'

Rex tutted angrily and slammed the van into reverse. The tyres screeched as he backed up the dirt track to the small circle of earth at the start of the run.

Dennis walked back to his position beside the track. He couldn't shake off the bad mood that had clung to him for most of the day. 'We'll go again in three minutes,' he called out to Rex and the assembled crew.

But Rex Lincoln wasn't the real cause of his anger – he was just the guy who happened to be there. It was the envelope burning a hole in his jacket pocket that was really getting to him. Its echoes of the past and tangles with the present were unnerving. Managing Rex Lincoln and the other stunt artists could be trying but it shrivelled in comparison to the family crisis that loomed over him. It had been brewing for months but now it was getting nearer and nearer to the crunch.

However much he didn't want to respond to the letter, he realised he had no choice. He needed to make a decision. Fast.

Venus got a lot of attention from the other girls when they realised she'd caught the vandal.

'You mean you rugby-tackled him to the ground? Wow! Weren't you frightened? What if he'd had a gun?'

'I've never seen anyone move so fast, Venus!'

Venus wasn't in the mood to talk about it, and thankfully Miss Sutton distracted the group by asking them to do some observational sketches that captured some of the complexities of the castle's architecture. Venus climbed over a ruined wall and sat on the steep grassy bank that led down to the moat. She wanted to be alone for a bit.

Her sketchpad was on her lap, but instead of drawing she chewed her pencil and mulled things over. After a while, she sensed a presence at her side. DC Summers crouched down beside her.

'What was all that about back there?' he asked. 'I heard one of the girls say you were chasing someone. Is that right?'

Venus nodded.

'Wanna tell me about it?'

Venus shrugged. 'I thought it was this boy called Franco. He's someone I came across in the summer holidays. DCI Radcliff knows all about him. I spotted him soon after we got here and then I saw him on the ramparts. I *had* to chase him. I needed to know what he was doing here.'

'But he's not connected to Tatiana – at least that's what Miss Sutton said you'd told her?'

'No, it's nothing to do with her.'

'So why the big chase? You're not supposed to be drawing attention to yourself.'

'It's complicated,' Venus muttered. She took the pencil out of her mouth and started sketching the drawbridge – a sign that the conversation was over.

Summers took the hint. 'OK,' he said, standing up. 'If you want to talk about it, I'm around.'

He smiled at Venus but she just nodded.

'Thanks,' she mumbled, trying as best as she could to block all thoughts of Franco from her mind.

Venus sat by herself on the coach journey back to Bertram's. Jaz and Geri asked her to come and sit with them at the back but she wasn't in the mood to chat. Tatiana had given her a sour smile when their eyes had briefly met but Venus had too many other things on her mind to respond.

She couldn't think about anything else except Franco; she couldn't get his sinister, twisted smile or those empty eyes out of her mind. She remembered how Franco had tried to crush her inside a phone box with a motorbike and the vicious way he'd lunged at her with a sword. She thought about how certain she'd been that it was him at the castle, and shivered. She needed to get a handle on this fear. The whole episode made her feel edgy.

After the coach deposited them back at Bertram's, Venus headed straight for her room, unwilling to talk to anyone about the day's events. She'd only just kicked her trainers off and locked the door behind her, when her mobile went.

Venus took a deep breath and answered.

'Venus.' It was DCI Radcliff.

'Yes?'

'I've just spoken to DC Summers. He said there was a bit of an incident at the castle today – something about you leaving the rest of the group.'

Venus said nothing.

'He mentioned the name Franco. What happened?' asked Radcliff. 'Did you see him at the castle?'

Venus slumped down on to her bed. 'I thought I did,' she replied, 'but it wasn't him.'

There was a short silence.

'Anyway,' said Radcliff, 'DC Summers told me you completely looked the Tatiana part, so well done. I'm less pleased with Ms Fairfleet, as it sounds as if she made no effort at all to disguise herself. That kind of ruins the plan, doesn't it?'

'Yeah,' agreed Venus. But at that moment she didn't really care about Tatiana Fairfleet or the whole body double thing.

'Right,' said Radcliff. 'Well, phone me immediately if anything else bothers you, OK?'

'I will do,' answered Venus.

* * *

Harding and Smiler crouched down behind a parked blue van. Once again, they were outside the back entrance of the huge mirrored building they'd staked out the night before.

They were carefully monitoring every move of the guard inside.

Harding checked his watch. This was the time the guard had taken a break the night before. They'd been told that he was a man of strict routines and their informant seemed to be right. At the start of his break yesterday, he'd appeared further up the pavement, on the corner of the street. He'd smoked a single cigarette. He'd looked up at the night sky. But, more importantly, he'd left the front door open.

This was the key to their plan.

The guard's entire break had lasted five minutes which would just about give them time.

Sure enough, a minute later the guard emerged further down the street and lit up a cigarette, leaving the front door behind him propped open with a chair.

'OK,' hissed Harding. 'Go, go.'

Smiler dashed forward and pressed a tiny black metal box against the doors at the back of the building. Harding kept his eye on the guard, who was still looking the other way, blowing smoke rings in the air.

Smiler flicked a switch on the box. A green light appeared in a small window on the contraption, indicating that the building's alarm system was down. This was because the guard had left the door open. The second he finished his break and shut the door again, the alarm system would be reactivated and the colour on Smiler's box would turn from green to red. If they were still inside when this happened, they'd be in deep trouble.

Smiler pushed two buttons on his box. A small LED panel lit up and ran through a series of numbers until it reached zero. The back door clicked. Harding pulled it open. They were in.

They took the steps before them three at a time. On the third floor, they ran through a lobby. Smiler scanned a small plastic card through a metal groove in the wall in front of a set of double doors. The doors swung open.

They entered a huge open-plan office. The street lamps outside lit up parts of it, while other areas were shrouded in darkness. There were desks set up in a seemingly haphazard fashion. Their surfaces were crammed with empty coffee cups, stacks of files, computers, telephones and different coloured directories.

The men sped over to the last door on the left and nodded at each other as Harding eased it open. They hurried over to an enormous worktop that stretched the whole way across to the far side of the room. Beside the worktop was a series of filing cabinets. Smiler scanned the names on each cabinet and selected the third one along. His fingers drummed down the surface of this cabinet until they reached the second drawer from the bottom.

Harding held the cabinet door open as Smiler flicked through a series of files. He shook his head.

Beads of sweat trickled down both of their faces.

Harding checked his watch. They needed a quick result. Smiler moved on to the drawer above.

'No,' he mouthed silently after his fingers had flown through the files.

'Come on,' hissed Harding, his gaze rapidly switching between Smiler and the door and back again.

With the next drawer up, Smiler struck gold. He'd gone through about fifty files when he stopped. Pulling a pair of tweezers from his inside jacket pocket, he lifted something out and slipped it into a small envelope.

Harding gave Smiler the thumbs-up and hurried across to the other side of the room. He grabbed something bulky off a desk and nodded at Smiler.

Smiler eased the cabinet door shut and they began to retrace their steps.

But on re-entering the main office, they both immediately spotted a figure walking in through a side door.

'Down!' Harding commanded.

Both men fell on to their stomachs.

Smiler swore under his breath.

Harding stuck his head out beyond a space divider. It was one of the staff – a woman.

She flicked on a desk lamp and sat down.

Smiler looked anxiously at Harding.

'Leave it to me,' mouthed Harding.

Smiler nodded.

Harding quickly crawled down a narrow aisle to their left and when he reached the end, he made a meowing sound – an exact impersonation of his cat, Carlos.

The woman stood up immediately.

Please don't use the phone, Smiler prayed.

She walked cautiously towards the source of the cat sound. As soon as she was parallel with a nearby set of office divider walls, Harding and Smiler set off.

Crawling on all fours, they passed behind her and found themselves back at the door on the other side of the office. Smiler looked round for a second. The woman was switching on lights, looking under desks and making what she thought were cat-friendly greetings.

Smiler swiped the card again and they let the door close silently behind them. They hurtled down the stairs at lightning speed. Harding checked his watch. The five minutes were nearly up. The woman's appearance had put them back over thirty seconds. That time period could be crucial. In about ten seconds, they'd be stuck.

Smiler led the way as they pelted down the stairs.

There were five seconds left.

Smiler's hand came into contact with the back door and he punched it open. He jumped outside with Harding only centimetres behind him. Smiler hurriedly clicked the door shut. A split second later, the small LED on the box changed from green to red; the alarm system had been reactivated. They retrieved the box, crossed the road quickly and hurried away from the building.

It had been agonisingly close, but they'd got what they came for.

Venus found it hard to concentrate in the morning's first lesson – double maths. French wasn't any better, nor was history in the afternoon. She couldn't stop thinking about yesterday's episode at the castle.

OK, Venus, she told herself. *Get a grip. You thought it was Franco; it wasn't. He's no nearer to you than he was before the castle visit. Be vigilant but don't overplay this whole thing.*

After history Venus was walking back to Acc Block 2 with Geri and Jaz when she spotted Tatiana up ahead, walking towards them. Expecting her to just walk past them, they were all surprised when she stopped directly in front of them.

'Hi Geri, Jaz,' said Tatiana.

'Hi,' they both replied with shocked expressions on their faces, unsure why the aloof actress suddenly speaking to them.

Tatiana then turned to face Venus. 'Oh, and *hello*, Venus,' she added, with a fake Hollywood smile. 'How's the *school exchange* programme going?'

Venus winced, feeling as if the girl had just slapped her round the face.

'It's funny that you're only here for a week,' mused Tatiana. 'I mean, what can you achieve in a week? Or is there something else you're here for?'

Venus's fists nearly exploded.

What the hell is she playing at?

Being sour was one thing, but actually trying to undermine the body double project was outrageous.

Venus composed herself before replying.

'Yeah,' she said as coolly as she could. 'It's going fine. Maybe I'll recommend that you come to my school in return – give you a feel for what a tough comprehensive is like for a cosseted actress.'

Tatiana's cheeks abruptly reddened and she stared acidly at Venus.

'Getting a bit too up yourself, aren't you?' scowled Tatiana.

'No,' fired back Venus, 'just sticking to the plan.'

Tatiana looked at Venus sulkily.

Venus stared back.

Tatiana tutted a couple of times and then sauntered away.

Jaz and Geri slowly turned to face Venus.

'What was *that* all about?' asked Jaz, in amazement.

'Yeah,' said Geri. 'And what did you mean, sticking to the plan?'

Venus gulped but quickly recovered. 'I just meant that I'm settling down here, that's all.'

'But she spoke as if she knew you,' pointed out Geri.

Venus shrugged. 'That's what the film business must do to you. It makes you think you know everyone.'

Geri and Jaz were staring at her as if they didn't quite believe her.

'Has she been picking on you?' asked Jaz.

Venus relaxed a tiny bit and forced a smile.

'Nah,' she said. 'I just don't like arrogant people.'

'Well, I'll tell you one thing for certain,' said Geri. 'You just got more conversation out of Tatiana Fairfleet than any of us have ever done.'

'Yeah,' said Jaz, with a laugh. 'You should get a medal for getting her to talk to the plebs!'

Venus quickly stuck her nose haughtily in the air and put on her poshest voice. 'What can I say, girls? I'm a genius!' she said, and they burst out laughing.

Luckily Jaz and Geri had other things to do, because Venus wanted to clear her head. She walked towards the Sculpted Lawns. It was a warm evening with a light breeze. She'd done a long run early in the morning before breakfast and now she wanted something more like a leisurely stroll. There were a few younger girls sitting out on the lawns, chatting. Venus passed them and headed towards the tennis courts. She was just stepping out of a narrow avenue of bushes when she bumped into Mr Foster.

His face was a beetroot colour and he looked hassled.

'Watch where you're going!' he snapped, without looking at her.

Yourself, thought Venus. 'I didn't see you coming,' she explained.

'Oh it's you,' he said with disdain, as he looked up and saw her face. 'Are you snooping around again?'

Venus stared at him in irritation. She thought back to how he'd accused her of snooping on Sunday when she'd seen him through his office door. That was kind of understandable, but this was ridiculous. She was allowed to be here; she wasn't breaking any rules. The guy was totally paranoid and for some unknown reason seemed to hate her.

'I wasn't snooping,' she replied firmly.

'Well, I'm in a hurry,' he snapped, barging past her.

'Have a nice day!' Venus called out after him.

She watched him storm off down the path. He really did look as if a thundercloud had positioned itself above him and was refusing budge.

Talk about an overreaction! DC Summers must be a hero to work with him for a whole week.

Venus carried on walking, trying to put as much distance between herself and the grumpy, paranoid site manager as possible.

She tried to forget him and thought of Jed instead. He hadn't rung to set a new date for the weekend in London. *Should I text him?* As she walked back to the school her mind examined this question from every angle.

'Hey, Venus,' said Jaz with a smile, as she entered the Refectory. 'We were a bit worried about you. Tatiana seemed to really annoy you back there.'

'She did a bit,' Venus replied, 'but it's no big deal.'

'Cool,' said Geri. 'Did you go for your walk?'

'Yeah, I was thinking about Jed . . .'

* * *

After supper Venus hung out with Jaz, Geri, Daisy and Zaynab, in Geri's room. Geri had a great coffee machine and she made the five of them excellent cappuccino-type coffees.

'So what do you make of Bertram's so far?' asked Zaynab. 'Is it completely different from your school?'

That led to a conversation about boarding schools and what everyone missed most about home. Venus talked a bit about her mum – it turned out that Jaz's dad was also a lawyer and they wondered if the two of them knew each other. Venus said she'd never known her father and probably never would. The girls were sympathetic, but luckily they were too sensitive to question her further.

Venus waited for half an hour after L.O.

She opened her door and peered out.

The corridor was empty – no sign of Finchy anywhere.

She tiptoed stealthily down the corridor, stopped at the stairwell and listened. Silence breathed through the building. In a few seconds she was at the bottom of the stairs and had walked through the door into the quad. Moonlight skimmed the surface of cobbled stones. Venus looked up. Every light in the three Acc Blocks was off. However stupid everyone thought L.O. was, it simply wasn't worth the hassle of being caught by Finchy.

Venus hurried across the quad, went under the archway and stepped out on to the huge patio. She crossed it quickly and went down the steps on to the Sculpted Lawns.

Her destination was Mr Foster's office. He was really

bothering her. It wasn't just his paranoia or the way he'd told her off for nothing – she kept on remembering the phone call she'd overheard on Sunday: 'I've told you already that it will happen on Friday. It's all sorted. Just leave it with me.'

At the time this had meant nothing to her, but now his words seemed to take on an edgy chill. Could they mean something sinister? Might his telephone conversation be related in some way to Tatiana? She didn't know. It was probably crazy, but his nervy manner made her feel unsettled.

That was why she was going to break into his office tonight.

She could have just reported her suspicions to DCI Radcliff, but after the incident at Repton Castle, she felt she was on slightly shaky ground with the DCI. Radcliff might think she was completely crazy if she started hatching theories about Mr Foster.

No, she was going to deal with this herself. Whatever he'd been talking about, she'd feel much happier if she checked the office out. Yes, Radcliff would kill her if she found out, but Radcliff wasn't there. If there was anything incriminating in Mr Foster's office, then of course she'd report it to Radcliff. If it was clean she'd keep her mouth shut and never mention it to anyone – apart from Kate, of course.

She'd only walked a few paces across the Sculpted Lawns when a harsh voice sounded behind her.

'Is that you, Venus?'

Her heart sank. It was Finchy.

She turned round slowly.

'What on earth are you doing out here?' demanded the headmistress sharply. The moonlight lit up half of Mrs Finch's face. It looked ghostly and displeased.

'It's ten-thirty-five. L.O. took place ages ago. You know the rule.'

Venus opened her mouth to reply, but Mrs Finch held up a finger crossly.

'I don't want to talk about anything out here,' said Mrs Finch coolly. 'Go straight to my study. I need to finish my L.O. inspection and will be there in a few minutes.'

Venus was about to speak again, but Mrs Finch swished her hand to usher Venus away.

A minute later, Venus was inside the headmistress's inner sanctum.

Her study was vast. There was a spotless beige carpet, floor-to-ceiling bookshelves and an array of dark teak furniture. The centrepiece of the room was Mrs Finch's massive desk, which had probably taken ten rainforests to create. Venus walked across the room and stood by the desk. It had ornate wooden figures of birds and fish carved into its surface, and the drawer handles were lions' mouths.

She knew she should probably sit on the chair opposite Mrs Finch's, but curiosity latched its slender fingers round her and pulled her towards the headmistress's chair. She noticed three purple files nestling next to each other on the desk in front of it. One of them in particular grabbed her eye.

Finances it said on the front.

Leave it, screamed a voice in her head. *Open it,* screamed another one.

Venus checked the door.

Should I or shouldn't I?

Oh, what the hell – go for it.

She flicked through several pages, which were completely boring. But she stopped when she found a posh-looking letter with an embossed address in the top right-hand corner. She scanned the text with growing surprise.

It didn't make sense.

Did it?

She quickly read the letter again.

She'd just finished it when she heard the door handle turning.

Oh my God! It's Finchy!

If she'd been in trouble for flouting the L.O. rule, she'd be *dead* if she was discovered leafing through the head-mistress's files!

She slammed the file shut and leaped across the desk.

By the time Mrs Finch had entered the room, Venus had just managed to straighten up and stand demurely behind the chair on the opposite side of the desk.

'Well then, Venus,' said the headmistress, striding across the room. 'Are you going to tell me why you are up so late, breaking one of my most important school rules?'

Venus was ready for this, and launched straight into her plan.

She burst out crying.

'It's . . . it's just that I couldn't sleep because I'm feeling really homesick,' Venus blurted out, the tears streaming down her face. 'I know it's stupid, but I miss my mum and all of my friends.'

She wiped her nose with her jacket sleeve for good effect.

'It's all right,' said Mrs Finch, offering her a tissue and trying her hardest to conjure up some sympathy. 'Many of our girls get homesick at some stage. Maybe this whole thing is a bit much for you – not just being here, but your duties with regard to Tatiana Fairfleet. Perhaps I should call DCI Radcliff and tell her it's not working out?'

Venus wiped her face again and put the tissue in her jacket pocket.

'No,' she said much more calmly. 'I feel a bit better now I've had a cry. I'll be fine.'

'Are you sure?' asked Mrs Finch.

Venus nodded. The tears had miraculously dried up now.

Thank God for drama lessons at school! It's not Hollywood, but it's obviously done the trick.

THURSDAY

Venus closed her eyes for a second and let the night breeze blow over her face. It was cool up on the Acc Block roof.

Today, she'd sat through double English and geography in the morning and double art and French after lunch. She'd tried to focus but, as usual in this place, her mind wandered and she thought about Finchy catching her out last night. It had been annoying, but it wasn't going to stop her from trying to get into Mr Foster's office again.

The more she thought about it, the more she felt that Mr Foster wasn't all he appeared. He was involved in something, she was sure of it. His sulky manner bothered her deeply. He seemed to be a man with lots of things on his mind – not all of them related to the upkeep and security of this site. Tonight she'd get into his office without Finchy seeing her. Tonight, she'd be better organised.

During supper, she'd let slip that she was heavily into kickboxing and Geri and Jaz had begged her to teach them some moves. So after they'd finished eating they went up to Geri's room, pushed the bed against a wall and started their tuition. Venus showed them the attacking and defending stances and then exhibited some of the basic kicks. They were good students; they listened and tried hard. But realising it would take them a long time to perfect any of the moves, they asked Venus for more demonstrations and watched her with admiration; she clearly knew what she was doing.

Venus waited far longer after L.O. than the night before. And this time, instead of going straight out into the quad, she found a way out through a skylight window. That was how she came to be sitting on top of the roof when her mobile sounded. She answered it instantly, hoping no one had heard it.

'Hi, babes.'

Oh God, Mum! Quick, sound normal.

'Hey, Mum.'

'Why are you whispering?'

Venus kept the call short. She said she couldn't risk being overheard talking in her room by Mrs Finch and thankfully her mum accepted that.

The Acc Block roof was a flat section with three turrets to her left and the edge of Acc Block 3 to her right. Her vantage point gave her an excellent view of the quad, the patio, the Sculpted Lawns, the tennis courts and way beyond. She figured that if she stayed up here for a bit longer – carefully keeping an eye on things down below – there would be a much smaller chance of being caught by Finchy. Only then would she make her move on Mr Foster's office.

Finchy must surely stop her night wanderings at some stage. The woman must need to sleep some time.

Venus hugged her knees.

Her thoughts turned to Jed again and his cancelled visit. Apart from the disappointment she'd felt, there was another nagging worry. *What if he was lying about the visit of his Australian aunt and uncle? What if he'd made it up because he was going to spend that weekend with some other girl?*

Stop it, she commanded herself. *He's not that sort of boy. He likes me. Of course he's telling the truth. He said he'd reschedule the visit, didn't he? So he will. Don't worry.*

It was hard not to get emotionally twisted up in the whole thing. She looked out across the night sky, willing his Australian aunt and uncle to change their minds and postpone their visit.

She checked her watch.

Give it another five minutes and then go.

But before the five minutes expired, her eyes suddenly caught sight of two headlights in the distance, slowly snaking their way up the narrow, twisting drive that led up to the rear gates of the school, just beyond the tennis courts.

Venus tracked the lights steadily.

It could be one of the older girls getting a lift home from a trip to see her boyfriend, or a teacher returning from a pub or a restaurant. But why were they returning to the *back* gates of the school? There was a locked gate at the top of the back drive and nowhere to park. Plus they'd have to make it over the perimeter wall. This would be OK for Venus, but not for most other people.

So what was the car doing out there? Maybe it was Mr

Foster? He must have a set of keys to unlock the back gate. That was it. It would be Mr Foster.

This put Venus on edge. She'd been planning to get into his office, but if he was up and about and slinking through the grounds, it made the whole office-break-in far more dangerous.

As Venus watched, the two small discs of light came to a stop. Venus waited for the car to move forward again but it stayed put. A minute later, it was still stationary.

She rubbed her nose and thought. She was already suspicious of Mr Foster and now he was doing this. What was he up to? She needed to get down there and take a look. She waited another two minutes, but the car stayed where it was.

Venus stood up and pulled her jacket tighter. In one direction was the warmth and safety of her bed. In the other lay the cold unknown, Mr Foster's office and the dark school drive with its mysterious parked car.

The fire escape was the best option down.

Venus had ignored the risk-*averse* part of her brain and had instead gone with the risk-*taking* part. There was no point in using any of the stairways inside the building. If Finchy was still up, it would be playing right into her hands.

She reached the bottom of the fire escape and started running across the quad, looking all around as she went, checking for any signs of the prowling headmistress. She sped underneath the arch, over the patio and on to the Sculpted Lawns. She ducked behind a bush and looked back.

There was no sign of Finchy.

As she ran, the hedges and bushes looked like strange, swaying creatures with beady eyes and outstretched arms. She tucked her hair into the back of her jacket and pulled the collar up round her face. If any of the CCTV cameras picked her up, hopefully she wouldn't be recognisable.

She looked quickly in the direction of Mr Foster's log cabin office. It was nearer than the car and she could probably get in and out of there quicker than it would take her to check out his vehicle. But it was the car that intrigued her more so she followed her instincts. It would be nice to see what he was up to. Of course, he could just be smoking a cigarette while listening to the BBC World Service.

She ran alongside the tennis courts and stopped when she reached the high perimeter wall of the school – the one she'd pulled DC Summers off. She hit the wall at speed and got a foothold on a thin slab of jutting-out stone. Easing herself up on to the ridge, she realigned her feet before jumping down the other side. Her trainers hit the tarmac quietly.

Venus looked into the darkness of the rutted drive stretching ahead of her. She'd calculated that the car was a hundred metres away – it would only take her seconds to get there.

Then what? The plan is to get near the car, and find out what Mr Foster is up to. And then check out his office.

She climbed over a stile and started jogging down the field running parallel to the drive.

The drive was on her right, separated from the field by a towering, thick hedgerow. Venus reckoned she'd be able to see Mr Foster through the hedge but that he wouldn't be able to see her.

She ran at a good pace, keeping very close to the giant hedge, her body immediately tuned to her pace and stride length. Running was in her blood and veins. Dennis had been an excellent runner during his youth in Trinidad. He always said she'd inherited his athletic abilities.

As the thin beams of the car's headlights came into view through the hedge, Venus slowed down.

Silence was essential.

If it was nothing, she'd only need a quick peek, then she'd be gone. She crept forward until she was almost parallel with the car lights. Crouching down, she peered through the thick hedge.

She could see the round, smoke-like circles of dust illuminated by each headlamp. The car was a BMW, in immaculate condition. This was interesting. She hadn't noticed a car like this on the school site before.

She took another couple of steps until she was leaning right against the hedge. The car was now only a few metres away from her. Its doors and windows were closed, but she could see inside it.

Mr Foster was in there but he wasn't alone. There was someone else too. *Who could it be?*

Slowly and as quietly as she could, Venus pulled back a small section of the thick hedgerow to get an even closer look. All she could see were two silhouettes. She could hear the muffled sounds of a conversation but couldn't actually make out what they were saying.

The minutes ticked by and Venus checked her watch several times. *How long am I going to wait out here?*

She was debating with herself whether or not to return, when the driver's window was abruptly wound down and the glowing butt of a cigarette was tossed out. Thankfully, the smoker didn't close the window completely.

What struck her first was the fact that it was two males talking. *OK. Big deal. There's no rule saying that site managers can't have male friends or be gay.*

But as her ears analysed the voices, it was immediately clear that neither of them was Mr Foster's. Although she'd only heard him speak a couple of times, she was absolutely certain. *So who are these guys?*

Venus chewed her lip in thought. They were talking so quietly that she couldn't make out any individual words.

She turned round and looked up into the branches of an oak tree to her left. Venus had loved climbing trees since she could remember. Her mum wasn't so keen but Venus was a strong child and heights held no fear for her. She'd also spent several days with Dennis on the set of *The Scales of the Pharaoh*. Twice she'd climbed the enormous façade of Cleopatra's palace. Even with a safety harness, it had still been a terrifying but ultimately exhilarating experience.

It was a matter of seconds before she'd climbed halfway up the tree. Luckily the tree's branches were thick and strong. She crept along a particularly sturdy branch, which stretched out above the drive, near to the rear of the car.

Slowly she lowered her right foot, gripping the branch with both of her hands. She did the same with her left until she was hanging vertically down from the branch. In one swift move she let go of the branch, fell downwards, bent her knees and landed by the left rear side of the car.

She hardly made a sound. *Good. They didn't hear me.*

Keeping low, Venus crept forward a few paces until she was crouching down right beside the driver's door. The men were still talking, but now Venus *could* pick out a few words.

'Rendezvous . . . negative . . . approach.'

The conversation continued but a breeze brushed past Venus and she couldn't hear any more.

Well, if there's no useful sound, I'll have to get a visual.

Incredibly slowly, she raised her head, centimetre by centimetre, until her eyes were parallel with the very bottom of the driver's window.

Please don't let one of them turn to face me.

The men had gone silent, but now Venus had a thin layer of vision. She could see them. The man in the driver's seat was shining a torch on to an official-looking piece of paper. But no sooner had Venus seen it, than he started to fold it. Venus cursed her luck, but she had just managed to glimpse two words at the top of the paper – *Basildon Street.*

This road name meant nothing to her.

Who are these guys and what are they up to? Could they possibly be plotting to grab Tatiana? Are they working with Mr Foster? Or has the castle incident made me just that little bit paranoid and over-dramatic?

As Venus mulled all of this over, she decided it was time to head back. But she'd been so eager to get near the car that she'd forgotten to plan the logistics of her return. The oak tree was out of the question – the branch was far too high for her to reach. And she couldn't just push herself back against the hedgerow – the movement would attract their attention. OK, she'd get clear of the car, run down the drive until she found an opening and get back that way.

But as she edged backwards with painful slowness, her left trainer plunged into one of the many potholes in the road's surface. She slipped sideways, banging her shoulder against the car's bodywork.

'What the hell was that?' one of the voices in the car asked loudly.

Both car doors flew open and two pairs of boots thudded on to the surface of the drive.

'Over there!' hissed one of the men, his torch picking out a blurred silhouette.

'It's probably just an animal,' the second man said.

'It didn't look like one,' replied the first man, 'it was more like a person. You take the field, I'll take the road!'

Venus only had a few seconds' advantage.

Somehow she'd managed to squeeze herself through the smallest of gaps in the hedgerow.

Now she was running as if her life depended on it.

One of the men had obviously found his way through the hedge as well and he was racing after her.

Venus flew forward, the blood pounding between her ears, her heartbeat accelerating by the second.

Why are these guys coming after me?

True, she wouldn't like to be spied on if she was sitting, talking on a narrow country lane, late at night – but she wasn't sure she'd actually *chase* an eavesdropper. Unless what she was talking about was top secret.

The wet grass and weeds in the field scuffed against her trainers. She looked desperately to her left – the way back to Bertram's. It was too risky. The other guy could be running up the drive towards the school. If he was, he'd be able to cut her off. No, she had to go forwards. At the far end of the field was a fence that led on to another field. The field she was in had little cover but the second field had plenty of trees. She'd have much more of a chance to hide there and escape them.

Suddenly a torch beam swept in great arcs behind her – narrowly missing her outline. Venus felt shivers of panic over her body. The torch was bound to find her if she didn't quickly put some distance between herself and her chaser. But the man had longer strides than her and he was closing the gap second by second. If the other man joined him, she'd be for it. She needed to focus and use every scrap of strength she could muster. She didn't fancy being caught by them, whoever they were and whatever they'd been talking about.

The torch beam cut through the night sky again, skirting centimetres wide of her left foot. The man was gaining on her, his heavy boots trampling the ground.

Fear drove Venus on. She pushed herself for that extra speed and kept going straight, the fence by the second field coming nearer every second. But the man was still cutting down the distance between them.

His torch swung back across the field. Again it missed her by the tiniest of margins.

With its next movement it would be sure to pick her out.

If the man grabbed her, she didn't reckon that saying she'd just fancied a little night stroll would go down very well. These men were clearly agitated by her presence.

She pelted forward, but with the fence only about twenty metres away, she slipped on the wet grass and took a tumble to her left. Her body smacked against the ground and she rolled over.

The man's footsteps were nearly upon her.

There was no way she could escape his clutches now.

Why did I come out here? Am I mad? No heroics, Radcliff had said. NO HEROICS! Maybe she had been right.

The man tightened his clench on the torch and suddenly stopped. The sound of running feet had ceased abruptly.

He flashed the torch in small circles, checking the ground immediately surrounding him. When nothing was revealed, he made the sweep larger – moving the torch-beam over a greater distance. He was about to intensify his search, when he heard the other man calling out to him.

'Any joy?' came the voice.

'Nothing,' was the response. 'What about you?'

'Clear. Let's get away from here.'

'But they're somewhere very near!'

'Forget it. We need to go! Now!'

The man with the torch pulled an exasperated expression. Maybe it had just been an animal, albeit a pretty big one. But what kind of animal was big enough to slam into the car like that and yet small enough to get through such a little hole in the hedgerow? Angrily he flashed his torch in another arc and shook his head. The torch illuminated nothing other than stretches of grass, a pond and a line of trees. He swore under his breath. He'd been right on to whatever it was and now it had vanished from sight. How could that have happened? He'd been sure he was going to catch up with it. He kicked the grass with frustration and started back down the field towards the car.

Venus waited for ten minutes. She was shaking with cold and fear, but was immensely relieved she hadn't been found.

She was lying on her back in a shallow pond. It had been a desperate move in the seconds of panic that had gripped her after she'd fallen. She'd chanced on the pond in the darkness and had plunged straight in.

There was only about forty centimetres of water in the pond – just enough to cover all of her body except for her nose, so she could keep breathing while her body had been submerged. Unfortunately, the water in the pond was stagnant and freezing. Fortunately, she'd been able to keep her mouth closed.

Very slowly she stood up, her body-weight increased massively by the icy water clinging to her clothes and skin. She was freezing and she shook her whole body, like a dog. Now all she had to do was go back to the school, get in the Acc Block and return to her bedroom without anyone hearing or seeing her. Easier said than done, when every single footstep she took was a loud, squelchy affair.

As Venus headed back up the field towards Bertram's, she dialled Kate's mobile. Luckily her mobile was still working. The phone rang ten times before the voicemail message sounded. She cursed and left a message. She then dialled Radcliff's number, but her phone cut out before it made the connection. Venus could have hit herself – her phone was out of juice; she'd forgotten to charge it up.

Her body was shaking so much that it seemed to be ignoring her brain's directional control, lurching from side to side in jerky movements. She felt like she'd been entombed in a huge block of ice. She gritted her teeth and thought of the hot bath and warm bed that lay ahead.

All she had to do was get there.

Scaling the perimeter wall was a bit of a struggle. Her clothes dragged her down and made movement far harder than before. She left great soaking patches on the stonework but she eventually made it over and started tramping back past the tennis courts and across the Sculpted Lawns.

Her mind was working in a frenzy. *What have I just seen? What were the men doing there? And are they really connected to Mr Foster? I'll have to devote tomorrow night to getting into his office – there's no way I'm going to attempt it now.*

She crossed the quad, leaving a trail of soggy footprints in her wake. When she was at the school buildings, she heard a distant thud. *It must be the men's car backfiring!* She turned back quickly, just to check the quad again and to her horror, she saw a figure hurrying right across it – *towards her.*

She swore silently. Was it one of the men? Or Mr Foster?

But as she hurried towards the door of Acc Block 2, she flicked her head round again. It was Mrs Finch!

Does the woman have no life at all? How late does she carry on doing her post-L.O. trawl? Maybe she's one of those women who can get by with four hours' sleep a night.

The headmistress peered around in the darkness.

Venus felt her heart thumping as she clung to the shadows and edged her way to the foot of an Acc Block doorway.

Mrs Finch muttered something inaudible to herself, then went inside.

Two minutes later, Venus was back in her room. She locked the door quickly and refrained from turning on any lights. Knowing Finchy, she'd probably be back out there, using binoculars and thermal imaging to track down a potential L.O. breaker.

In a flash, Venus tore off all her wet clothes, dropped them into the bath, dried herself as best as she could, got into her pyjamas and leaped into bed, with a towel wrapped round her head. She didn't dare take a bath in case Finchy heard her.

Venus lay motionless for over an hour, until she dared venture out of her bed to charge her phone. Then she slipped back into bed. She fell asleep wishing she could have a bath.

Her dreams that night were full of giant trees and dark hedgerows and deep, deep pools of water.

FRIDAY

In spite of her late bedtime, Venus woke early. The second she opened her eyes, the whole of the night before jolted back into her head: the men in the car, the chase, the soaking trail of footprints and the close call with Finchy.

She got up and looked into the en-suite. Her drenched clothes were in the same position she'd left them – bunched up together in the bath. She then remembered her phone. She grabbed it from the charger and speed-dialled Radcliff.

The DCI took a while to answer and when she did her voice sounded a bit rough. 'Venus?'

'I had a weird experience last night.'

'Hang on a second.'

Venus heard a shuffling sound.

'OK, tell me about it.'

It took Venus ten minutes to bring the DCI up to speed.

The DCI sighed. 'I did tell you not to put yourself in any danger, Venus,' she said.

'But what about the guys on the drive?' asked Venus. 'It sounds fishy, doesn't it? Do you think they're connected to any kidnapping plot?'

'I'm not sure,' replied the DCI. 'But I'm going to put two

more officers right outside the place you're visiting today. I'll also liaise with security there and ask them to keep a particular eye on your group.'

'That makes sense,' replied Venus.

'Good,' agreed Radcliff. 'But Venus?'

'Yeah?'

'I mean what I say. No more heroics. Just look like Tatiana and concentrate on the trip. Be aware of these security arrangements but don't focus too much on them. Got it?'

'Yes,' answered Venus.

'Right. Have a good trip.'

'Cheers.'

When Venus appeared at breakfast as a Tatiana Fairfleet look-alike again, Jaz and Geri stared at her in surprise.

'Hey, Venus,' called Jaz. 'Once is funny, but twice is weird. What's going on?'

'Yeah,' piped up Geri. 'Are you searching for work at a look-alike agency?'

'I just love winding up the prima donna,' Venus said with a grin.

Jaz and Geri giggled.

'All right, all right,' said Geri, 'we get the picture. Anyway where do you reckon we're going today?'

'Dennis Spring speaking.'

'Dad, it's me.'

'Hi, Gail.'

'Is everything all right?'

'Yes. Why?'

'It's just you sounded a bit edgy when I spoke to you last. Is there something on your mind?'

'No, nothing at all. I'm fine. It's just work pressure.'

'Your stunt team getting you down?'

'It's not the team; it's just Carly Fisher. I'm tired of her gung-ho attitude. She doesn't seem to care if she gets blown to bits or mowed down by a tank; safety is her last priority.'

'That sounds terrible,' Gail replied soothingly. 'Why doesn't she listen to you?'

Dennis sighed. 'She only listens when she wants to. But she seems to have all sorts of other things on her mind. If she doesn't pick up her game I might have to sack her.'

'Isn't that a bit dramatic?' asked Gail.

'Yeah – but sometimes there's no alternative.'

'All right, Dad, but don't stress yourself out about it too much.'

'No, it's all in hand. I've just had to do a lot of shouting.'

'*You? Shouting*?' said Gail, laughing. 'Never!'

'I know, I know. I'll tone it down a bit.'

'Good. All of this stress is bad for your heart.'

'Yes, kid, I get the picture.'

'And don't call me kid.'

'OK.' Dennis managed a chuckle.

'You promise me nothing's up?'

'Yep – really, love. Everything's fine.'

'Good. Got to go now, Dad. I've got to be in court in an hour.'

'Good luck, sweetheart.'

'Cheers, Dad. Look after yourself and speak to you later.'

Mrs Finch was reading a letter when there was a knock on her study door.

'Come in,' she called.

The door opened and Mr Foster walked in. He strode across the carpet, stopping some way in front of her desk.

'Good morning, Mr Foster,' she said. 'How can I help you?'

Mr Foster shuffled uncomfortably on the spot. 'I need to leave the site for a while this morning,' he said.

'Oh!' replied the headmistress with surprise. 'I thought we'd agreed that you were going to repair the tennis-court fences this morning.'

Mr Foster's cheeks broke out in tiny streaks of red. 'I won't be able to do that until I've bought some items from the DIY store in town, so I thought I'd do that this morning.'

Mrs Finch frowned for a few seconds, but then her face brightened a measure. 'So be it,' she said with a nod. 'I'll look forward to seeing you in the afternoon then?'

'Yes, Headmistress.'

With that, Mr Foster turned on his heels and hurried back towards the door.

Mrs Finch shook her head. She was sure that when they'd spoken about fixing the tennis-court fences last week, he'd told her that he already had all of the resources he needed.

* * *

Venus knelt by the side of the coach, doing up the laces on her trainers. All of the other girls were already on board, apart from her and Tatiana, who was now ambling towards her. DC Summers was a discreet distance behind Tatiana.

As Tatiana approached she hissed quietly, 'I don't know why you're bothering to try and look like me still. I told you – you can't be a body double because you don't look anything like me. Nice try and everything, but in the end, I reckon, a failure.'

Venus had just about had enough of Tatiana's attitude.

'Look,' she snapped back. 'I'm doing you a favour here. The least you could do is make some effort to dress down. I'm out of here on Sunday and after that I'll never have to see your spoiled face again.'

'Ooh,' goaded the actress, 'temper, temper.'

Venus ignored this wind-up and climbed on to the coach. She heard DC Summers ask Tatiana what their exchange was all about, but Tatiana didn't bother to answer the question.

Venus sat in the vacant seat across the aisle from Geri and Jaz, fuming.

Thirty minutes later, Miss Sutton stood up at the front of the bus as it pulled into a large car park.

'OK, girls,' she announced. 'As you can see, today we're visiting the recently opened Signature Technology Museum.'

Venus looked out of the coach window.

The museum was a huge, steel dome with four smaller circular pods leading off from it, each painted in Day-Glo colours: one red, one green, one yellow, one blue.

'We're going to the Future Communication Experience first,' explained Miss Sutton. 'It's situated in the red pod – known as the Zenith building. The exhibition is about ways we might communicate in a hundred years' time. It starts with a ten-minute film and then moves on to loads of inter-active stations; the whole thing's supposed to be brilliant.'

The girls on the coach stood up and grabbed their bags from the overhead storage shelves.

Venus watched Tatiana get off the coach. She wanted to put as much space as possible between herself and the nightmarish actress.

DC Summers was right behind Tatiana. Any nearer and he'd have been surgically attached to her.

The two plain-clothes officers sitting inside the unmarked Ford Mondeo across the road watched the Bertram's girls disappear inside the red Zenith building.

DC Steve Catterick and DC Alan Jensen nodded at each other in satisfaction.

Catterick made a quick call on his radio. 'They're in,' he said briskly, before turning to Jensen. 'Coffee?' he enquired. 'There's a café inside – I checked it out on the Internet.'

Jensen grinned and shook his head. Catterick could never go for too long without his caffeine fix.

Catterick stepped out of the car and strolled over to the museum's grey, main building. Jensen checked the entrance to the Zenith building again. Nobody had fol-lowed the Bertram's girls inside. No one was hanging around outside. It felt like the coast was clear. And DC

Summers was inside with them – he'd keep his eye on the ball. Jensen stretched over, reached inside the glove compartment and pulled out a newspaper.

The opening film on the possibility of brain downloads ended twelve minutes later, and the lights came on in the small auditorium.

Within a couple of seconds of adjusting her eyes to the light, Venus scanned the room and noticed immediately that Tatiana Fairfleet wasn't there.

She instantly saw that DC Summers had spotted this too. He looked wildly around the auditorium, stood up and hurried over to Venus.

'Did you see where she went?' he whispered urgently.

Venus shook her head.

'What's going on?' asked Geri, wandering over to them.

'I'll be with you in a sec, Geri,' replied Venus.

'OK,' said Summers anxiously. 'I'll go through the exhibition halls, you check outside. We need to find her, now.'

Miss Sutton observed this interchange and wondered what was going on as she saw Venus run out of the auditorium and push open an emergency exit on her left. Venus found herself on a narrow, tarmac path that curved round to the front of the Zenith building. She sprinted round the corner, arrived back in the car park and breathed a huge sigh of relief.

However much she disliked Tatiana, she was delighted to see the actress. She was way over on the other side of the car park, facing away from Venus, leaning against the side of the coach and making a furtive call on her mobile. She had probably sneaked out of the auditorium the second the lights went down.

As Venus started walking across the car park, turning her mobile on, her relief turned to anger. Tatiana was stupid to have gone off like this. It compromised the whole operation to keep her safe; she really was the most self-centred person on the planet.

Venus's phone beeped to announce the arrival of a text:

V sorry didn't get back 2 u last night – was @ party – didn't hear mobile. Checked out main batch of Basildon Streets – nothing. Then checked Basildon Street Central London – high profile companies on the street are: magistrates court, Landis Steel, Renton Computers, The Daily Enquiry + Althorp Defence Corp (they make guns). Hope this is useful – love K x.

Venus read the text again as she stepped across the gravel of the car park. Althorp Defence Corp – a company making guns? This struck a chord of alarm in Venus. Had the two men on the drive been connected in some way with guns? Were they gun-runners or something?

Venus heard Tatiana laugh about something.

Just get her back inside, Venus instructed herself.

'I don't believe it,' whispered Harding as he and Smiler watched Tatiana Fairfleet leaning against the coach and chatting on her mobile.

The two men had seen the man getting off the coach after

Tatiana when the Bertram's girls arrived. Save wearing a hat proclaiming *I AM A POLICEMAN*, he couldn't have made his profession more obvious. Harding and Smiler had also spotted the car parked on the other side of the road with two plain-clothes guys inside. One had sloped off when the girls went into the building; the other one was in the car, reading a newspaper. This had thrown Harding and Smiler – they hadn't expected Tatiana to be guarded.

Harding and Smiler's black Peugeot was parked between two large coaches and thus difficult to see. The plan was to grab Tatiana as the girls got back to the coach. Smiler would create a diversion while Harding would snatch Tatiana and get her into the Peugeot. Smiler would then join them in the car and they'd be off in less than five seconds.

But now here was Tatiana Fairfleet – alone, away from the rest of the group and without her police shadow.

It was almost too good to be true.

Harding nodded at Smiler. 'Let's do it,' he said.

As Venus closed in on Tatiana, she thought of DC Summers. *He'll be freaking out by now.*

She wished she had his mobile number so that she could text him and let him know that Tatiana was OK. She upped her pace. She needed to steer Tatiana straight back into the building and put DC Summers's mind at rest.

Venus was twenty metres away from Tatiana when two men suddenly sprang out from behind the coach and grabbed her. One was tall, the other much smaller. The tall one had his hand over Tatiana's mouth so she couldn't scream. The small one peeled away, leaped into a car and turned on the engine.

Venus's body jolted with shocking force.

OH MY GOD!

She started running.

NO! NO! NO! THIS ISN'T HAPPENING!

'STOP!' she yelled at the top of her panic-stricken voice, as her legs propelled her forward.

DC Jensen dropped his paper when he heard someone shout 'STOP!'

He looked over to the source of the noise. It had come from the museum car park across the road.

He instantly saw what was happening. One man was dragging Tatiana Fairfleet into a Peugeot. Another was in the driver's seat, gunning the car's engine.

In one movement Jensen was out of the car and flying across the road.

Venus crossed the car park in less than ten seconds. In that time, the taller man had already managed to get Tatiana into the back of the car. She must have been locked in because she was banging frantically on the window, letting out muffled screams.

In desperation, Venus leaped forward, her right foot lifted high and smashing against the side of the taller man's head.

He reeled backwards, but didn't fall.

'What the hell?' he yelled.

'Oh my God!' shouted the smaller man, jumping out of the car and gazing in stupefied horror at Venus. 'There are TWO of them!'

Venus spun round and kicked the smaller man in the stomach. He doubled over in pain.

'STAY STILL!' a third male voice yelled.

Venus saw another man running towards them. *Who the hell is he? Is he one of them? Or is he one of the plain-clothes guys?*

Tatiana's screams were getting louder and more hysterical.

The taller man lunged for Venus, but she dodged out of the way and managed to land a punch on the back of his shoulder.

'DON'T MOVE!' shrieked the man running towards them. 'I'M A POLICE OFFICER! DO NOT MOVE!'

Venus's question had just been answered.

She was about to hit the taller man again when she felt something small and cold against the back of her head. There was no mistaking the click of the safety catch.

'It's a gun. Now get in the car,' hissed the smaller man.

'BACK OFF!' yelled the taller man at the policeman. 'I SAID, BACK OFF! NOW!'

DC Jensen stopped in his tracks. 'OK, guys,' he said hoarsely. 'Let's take this easy. Let's calm down. It's going to be OK. I want you to put the gun down.'

Venus was tempted to struggle further, but decided against it when she saw the anguish on Tatiana's face and felt the hard metal against her head. A further attack on the tall guy was too risky.

'It's all right,' DC Jensen continued, edging forwards a

few steps. 'We can sort this out. But I want you to put the gun down first.'

'One more step and she gets a bullet in the head. Do you want that?'

DC Jensen froze.

In a flash, the small man grabbed Venus by the arm, pulled open the car's back door and shoved her roughly inside. She fell against a screaming Tatiana Fairfleet.

'STOP!' shouted DC Jensen, breaking into a run again.

The taller man threw himself into the back next to Venus while the small man leaped back into the driving seat and slammed his foot down on the accelerator.

DC Jensen threw himself forward and managed to grab on to the driver's door handle. But the Peugeot powered ahead. Jensen tried to hang on but he was hurled sideways and was dispatched forcefully on to the gravel. He watched in horror as the Peugeot sped away. 'NO!' he yelled.

Just then, he heard the screech of more tyres as a car swerved across the car park gravel and stopped centimetres from his body.

'Get in, Jensen!' It was DC Catterick in the Mondeo.

A stunned Jensen dragged himself off the ground and sprung into the passenger seat.

'What happened?' demanded Catterick as he hit the accelerator.

'They came from nowhere!' yelled Jensen.

'Put your seatbelt on!' urged Catterick.

Jensen slammed the passenger door shut and grabbed

his seatbelt. He then reached for the blue light on the dash-board, stuck his hand out of the window and clamped it on to the roof. The light immediately began to flash and the siren started howling.

DC Jensen was shaking as he grabbed his radio and pulled it close to his mouth. 'Armed abduction in progress,' he barked frantically. 'Target is Tatiana Fairfleet. Repeat, Tatiana Fairfleet plus body double. Assailants are two IC1 males, one armed with handgun. Immediate armed assistance required. Suspects are driving a black Peugeot sedan, index: lima charlie five foxtrot tango five. Giving chase on B771. Repeat, armed assistance required.'

DCI Radcliff was putting the finishing touches to a Powerpoint presentation when her desk phone rang. She put a thick pile of notes to one side of the desk, dragged her eyes away from the computer screen and picked up the receiver.

'What is it?' she barked. 'I'm preparing for a meeting.'

'It's Tatiana Fairfleet,' responded the voice on the other end of the line. 'She and her body double have been abducted.'

Radcliff felt like someone had just slapped her in the face. In the stunned seconds after she dropped the phone, she managed to grab her coat and snatch her keys off the desk before running out of the office.

'Harding, what the hell's going on?' shouted the small man from the driver's seat. 'How can there be two of them?'

'It doesn't matter,' shouted Harding. 'Just drive!'

'Of course it matters!' hissed Smiler anxiously.

'It doesn't!' screamed Harding.

Harding, Venus and Tatiana were squashed into the back seat, Harding's gun still pressed against the side of Venus's head. Tatiana was screaming hysterically.

'Shut it!' snarled Harding at Tatiana.

Tatiana gulped back her sobs. Her whole body was shaking in frenzied jumps.

Venus couldn't believe this was happening. Radcliff's informant had been correct. And she recognised these men's voices – they were the ones who'd been talking in the car on the school drive.

She turned her head a centimetre; the tip of the gun felt harsh and cold. Fear was creeping through her body, hot on the heels of shock. In spite of her kickboxing abilities, there was no way she could overpower *both* of the men in the car. One slip of Harding's finger, the gun would go off and she'd be dead. She needed to get them outside but these two guys didn't look like chancers; they'd been there in the car park, waiting. *How on earth had they known the trip's destination? Someone must have told them, but who?*

'Put your foot on it, Smiler,' Harding commanded. 'Lose that lot.'

The siren screamed behind them.

Venus couldn't move her head round to see how far the police car was behind them. Venus cursed herself and DC Summers. They'd both been in that darkened auditorium and they'd not noticed Tatiana leave. How much more stupid could they have been? But the main thrust of her anger was directed at Tatiana; the infuriating girl had sneaked away and for what? Probably for some pathetic phone call to one of her spoiled actress friends.

The Peugeot sped forwards. It reached the end of the road on which the museum was situated. Smiler turned left on to another road. They flew along this for about fifty metres and then he pulled the wheel down to the right. The car swerved around a corner and a national speed-limit sign flashed by. They were now on a narrow country road, and within seconds were going over a hundred miles per hour.

'Faster!' growled Harding.

The siren screeched behind them.

Tatiana's face was ashen with shock.

Harding turned towards the girls. 'Empty your pockets,' he commanded.

Venus and Tatiana did as they were told and handed the contents over. 'Is that everything?' Harding asked.

The girls nodded.

The first thing Harding did was to take the sim cards out of their phones and snap them in half.

Venus winced.

Smiler checked his rear-view mirror again. 'They're gaining on us!' he shouted as the wailing siren crept further towards them.

But at that second, from a concealed entrance in a field, a small white box van started pulling out on to the road.

'Speed up!' yelled Harding.

The van edged out further. It was now almost halfway across the road.

'We've got to make it!' barked Harding.

Smiler pressed his foot down on the accelerator pedal with all of his strength.

They'd never make it. They were going to smash right into the van.

But the Peugeot hit the left bank of the road. Its two left tyres jolted upwards and the car flew past the van, the tinny scrape of metal on metal screeching as it passed by.

'No!' yelled DC Catterick, leaning his head out of the Mondeo window. 'Police! Get out of the way!'

But the driver of the white van was struggling with the gears.

'Reverse!' shrieked Jensen.

'Get back in the field!' shouted Catterick.

Finally the van started reversing, but at an agonisingly slow pace.

Catterick thumped the dashboard with his fist. 'Move!' he shouted.

Finally, the van cleared the way and the Mondeo crunched forward. But after it had rounded two sharp bends, it came to a T-junction.

Catterick and Jensen looked left then right. There was absolutely no sign of the Peugeot.

'Which way?' Catterick shouted furiously.

'Dunno,' answered Jensen.

'I'm going right,' announced Jensen.

The Mondeo turned right, which was a poor choice, because the Peugeot had turned left. And therefore, as Smiler continued to drive at lightning speed, Venus and Tatiana were being taken further and further away from the Mondeo, from the policemen, and from safety.

Venus had been scared before: she'd escaped from a burning building, leaped off a plane carrying a canister of poison; she'd even nearly killed Franco. But the terror she felt at that moment – being enclosed with no options, and sitting next to a man holding a gun – was worse than any of those times.

There's absolutely nowhere to go.

These two guys, Harding and Smiler – presumably not their real names – have at least one gun. Does Smiler have one too?

Her thoughts were interrupted by Harding's gruff voice. 'Keep your foot on the pedal,' he told Smiler. 'They'll have the helicopter out soon. I want to be under cover before it's airborne.'

Venus's mind was spinning. How was she going to get herself and Tatiana away from these guys?

Smiler spun the car round a tight corner, drove a couple of hundred metres on a small country road and screeched to a halt in a lay-by where a blue BMW was parked.

'Get out!' Harding commanded. He eased out, pointing the gun at Venus all of the way. 'And no kickboxing tricks from *you*!'

Venus then got out, glaring at Tatiana. Tatiana started sobbing again. Harding turned towards her for just a second.

It was the second Venus needed.

She sprung forward and high-kicked out fiercely with her right foot. Her aim was perfect. Her foot crashed against Harding's arm. The gun careered out of his hand and flew into a patch of long grass on the bank at the side of the road. As Harding yelled out, Venus gave a thunderous kick with her left foot on the back of his calves. He crumpled on to the ground on his hands and knees.

Venus leaped over his body and pulled open the back door. 'Get out!' she screamed at Tatiana. 'Move!'

Tatiana responded instantly, tumbling out of the car. Venus grabbed her and helped her to her feet.

Smiler pushed his door open but Venus was ready for him and slammed it with her foot. It flew back against his shins. He howled in pain.

'STOP, YOU TWO!' Harding shouted, pulling himself to his feet.

But Venus and Tatiana were already ten metres away, fleeing into the field at the side of the road.

'Get the gun!' barked Harding, cursing violently. He took off after them, while Smiler dived into the grass to retrieve the weapon.

'This way!' yelled Venus to Tatiana.

The two of them pelted down the field. The grass hadn't been mowed for a while and it was interspersed with nettles and weeds, hampering their escape.

'Come on!' screamed Venus, tugging at Tatiana's elbow.

There was a metal gate at the far end of the field.

Venus looked round. Harding was right behind them. Smiler had located the gun and was running towards the car and getting back in. The tyres shrieked as he sped off.

'Over the gate!' she shouted at a panting Tatiana.

Venus jumped forward. Her hands pressed against the top of the gate and lifted her body, propelling her over it in one move. Tatiana climbed the first couple of rungs and threw herself over too.

'Hurry!' Venus implored her.

They were now on a narrow path with a high barbed wire fence on either side.

They kept going but Tatiana wasn't the fastest of runners. *She's going to get us caught if she doesn't move it!*

Up ahead was a series of metal buildings – they looked like storage sheds of some sort. Facing the girls was a rusty ladder that led up to the roof of the first building.

There was nowhere else to go.

Venus leaped on to the first rung and frantically began climbing. Tatiana grabbed the ladder beneath her and started climbing too. But Harding was right behind her. As she scuttled up, he flew forward and managed to grab her left trainer.

'Get off!' Tatiana screamed. 'Let go!' Hysteria and fear spiked her screams.

Venus looked down. Harding was yanking at Tatiana's left foot. Venus made her decision in less than a second. She swivelled her body round and jumped, her feet landing on Harding's back. He crashed sideways on to the ground – his right shoulder smashing against a large boulder. He groaned in pain, but Venus didn't give him another look. She was straight back on to the ladder.

Tatiana had reached the top and Venus quickly joined her on the smooth, flat roof.

'Let's go,' said Venus.

They ran forward together. Twenty metres later they stopped abruptly. The roof ended. There was no ladder here – just a two-metre jump on to the flat roof opposite them. The drop was at least two storeys.

'We've got to jump,' urged Venus.

'Oh my God,' whispered Tatiana.

'We *have* to,' insisted Venus.

'I don't know if I can,' hissed Tatiana in terror, looking at the ground below.

'Look, there's no choice,' snapped Venus.

She strode back several paces, dragging Tatiana with her.

'OK,' Venus said. 'Now!'

They ran forward together.

Venus jumped.

But Tatiana didn't. To Venus's horror she found herself flying forward, alone, on to the roof of the facing building.

Tatiana stood shakily by the edge of the drop, looking down in terror.

'Come on, Tatiana!' screamed Venus. 'Please! It's not that far! You can do it!'

At any moment, Harding was going to reappear behind Tatiana. But there was no sign of him yet. *Maybe I put him out of action when I kicked him off the ladder,* Venus hoped.

Tatiana trembled and took a few steps backwards.

'Stay where you are!' commanded a voice.

Venus spun round.

It was Smiler.

He'd managed to get up on the roof where Venus was standing. He was holding the gun steadily and pointing it straight at her.

'Right you,' he snarled at Venus. 'I don't care if you're Tatiana Fairfleet or not. All I care about is you jumping back over that gap and joining your twin sister.'

Venus looked over at Tatiana.

Behind her, Harding now emerged from the top of the ladder with a vicious look on his face.

Reluctantly, and with an enormously heavy heart, Venus jumped back through the air and landed next to Tatiana.

'Move back a bit!' shouted Smiler.

They moved back.

Holding on to the gun, Smiler cleared the gap himself and after his successful landing, he tightened his grip on his weapon.

'Right,' shouted Harding, resuming his leadership, his eyes burning with fury. 'I want them in the car, NOW!'

DC Jensen and DC Catterick had turned back after agreeing the girls hadn't gone down the road they'd taken, and ten minutes later, swore simultaneously as they approached a lay-by.

The black Peugeot was there.

Venus, Tatiana and the two men were not.

'No!' shouted Catterick. 'They've switched cars!'

'The DCI will kill us,' said Jensen quietly.

'I shouldn't have gone to get that coffee,' rued Catterick.

'I should have had my eyes on the car park instead of reading the paper,' muttered Jensen.

They sat in silence, the smell of grass cuttings and fresh hay wafting into their nostrils.

'They'll have the chopper over here in no time,' said Jensen optimistically. 'It might pick them up.'

Catterick shrugged his shoulders despondently.

'What are we going to do?' asked Jensen.

'We'd better head back,' replied Catterick, 'and face the music.'

'OK, you can sit up now,' said Harding testily.

After the men had recaptured the girls, they'd blindfolded them and stuck them in the back seat of the BMW. Harding had sat by them with his gun against Venus's right temple the whole way.

They sat up and Harding took off their blindfolds. Venus saw they were inside some sort of garage.

'Get out!' ordered Harding, gesturing with the gun.

They gingerly climbed out of the car. Harding held the gun against Venus's back. He wasn't going to be hoodwinked by her again.

The place smelled damp and musty. There was a hint of engine oil and discarded rags.

Smiler opened the boot quickly and pulled out a holdall containing something silver. But Harding saw Venus looking at it and jerked her roughly away.

'Leave the spare one in there,' commanded Harding.

For a second, Venus managed to see something black and shiny glint in Smiler's hand. He reopened the passenger door of the BMW and put something back inside.

Harding pulled Venus forward; Smiler took Tatiana and marched the girls to a blue door at the back of the garage. Its paintwork was cracked and peeling.

Harding opened the door. It led straight out to a corridor. They walked along this to the bottom of a cold stairwell.

'Move!' ordered Smiler.

The four of them climbed three flights of stairs. The stairwell walls were painted dark green; the doors leading off it were a bright red. Venus spotted a faded iron plaque on one of the stairwell walls; *Hawton Mill Warehouse*. She committed the words to memory.

At the top of the third flight, they stopped in front of an unmarked red door. Smiler punched a code into a battered security panel and they entered. Inside was a huge empty space. It must have been an office at one stage because there were some desks pushed against the walls, three space dividers in the centre of the room and some odd bits of computer equipment lying around. A discoloured calendar three years out of date hung off a pillar.

They were ushered into a small square room that was completely empty save for a very old, tatty wooden desk against one of the side walls. It had seen far better days. Its wood was splintered and cracked, a large nail protruding from its surface. Venus instantly noticed that there were no windows in the room.

Harding and Smiler stood in the doorway, eyeing the girls suspiciously. There was silence for a good few minutes.

'So what's the set-up?' asked Harding with a sneer. 'Which one of you is Tatiana Fairfleet?'

Venus and Tatiana said nothing.

Harding's grasp on the gun's trigger tightened.

'I *said* which one of you is Tatiana Fairfleet?' His voice was taut and angry.

Still the girls said nothing.

Smiler flicked his eyes nervously at Harding. 'I don't like it,' he muttered.

Harding growled. 'My friend here doesn't like the fact that you're not telling us what we want to know. He gets very edgy when people don't do what he says. And when *he* gets edgy I have a tendency to *shoot people*, to make him less edgy. So I'm going to repeat the question. *Which one of you is Tatiana Fairfleet?*'

'I am,' answered Venus and Tatiana at exactly the same second.

Smiler twitched nervously. Harding's stare hardened. He looked from Venus to Tatiana and back to Venus again.

'You know what,' he finally said, 'if you want to play this stupid game, go ahead. It doesn't matter. It won't affect our plans at all. Either way, you're not getting out of here. And remember, girls, don't try anything stupid. You can scream if you want, but . . .' He waved the gun round the windowless room. '. . . no one will hear you.'

Smiler opened his mouth nervously, but Harding raised the gun further in the air.

'We're out of here,' said Harding, nodding for his colleague to leave the room too. Right on cue, Smiler scampered out and Harding was right behind him.

Venus and Tatiana listened as three bolts were slid shut and two locks clicked.

They heard the men's footsteps fade away.

They were alone.

Tatiana slumped to the floor and buried her head in her hands. The sobs followed quickly.

Venus rubbed her eyes. *Tatiana can sit there and cry as much as she wants; she's an actress – she's good at it. And she got us into this mess in the first place. Why did she have to creep away from the museum to make a phone call? Why hadn't she taken Radcliff's advice more seriously? She's behaved the whole week as if she'd never even spoken to the DCI about a plot to kidnap her. Why couldn't she get over her film starlet persona for a few minutes and have heeded some advice? She is so damn arrogant and stupid.*

The room was airless and stuffy; only a very small draft of air stirred from under the door.

One word screamed in Venus's head: ESCAPE.

She grabbed the door handle and twisted it. It moved in her hands and so she pressed her right shoulder against it: nothing – not even the slightest budge. Those bolts and locks had looked pretty chunky from the outside.

She started to pace the room.

OK, so there's no window. I've got to think outside the box. I've got to get out of here. I suppose I have to get her out too, but at this minute I'd be more than happy to leave her here for ever.

She walked over to the old, broken wooden desk. Its white paintwork was scratched and faded, its surface dotted with hundreds of tiny indentations, like the pock-marks left on an adult's face after suffering from years of teenage acne.

There were six drawers in the desk, each one hanging out. Venus checked them all. They were empty. She thought for a moment about using one of them as a weapon, but the wood was so old and rotten that it would probably disintegrate on impact. She tried to move the desk, but it stood rigid. Each of its legs was fixed to the floor with screws.

She swore – letting out some of the fear and frustration.

Tatiana looked up for a second and wiped the tears from her eyes.

Venus looked away and went over to perch on the desk.

It looked like the number of escape routes was zero.

They were stuck in there.

'There!' pointed Radcliff – her shout just about audible above the deafening noise of the propeller.

The police helicopter swooped and flew over a line of trees. A massive expanse of woodland stretched into the distance.

Radcliff checked her map. Beyond the woodland was open land and then a series of large industrial parks.

She felt an anxious metallic squeeze in her chest. Her worst nightmare had just come true. The tip-off had been right. She should have taken her instincts even more seriously and devoted more manpower to the job. For God's sake – Dennis Spring's granddaughter was down there somewhere! How could she have exposed Venus and that infuriating actress to this? And how on earth was she going to break the news to Dennis? He'd said he was worried about the possible dangers of the job and she'd just brushed his concerns away. If anything happened to Venus, her life wouldn't be worth living.

The ports and airports had been alerted and Radcliff thought it virtually impossible for the kidnappers to get the girls out of the UK. No, they had to still be in the country and, most likely, holed up close by.

'What do you want to do?' shouted the pilot.

'Take it even lower,' Radcliff said.

The helicopter dipped until it was only about ten metres above the tops of the tallest trees.

Radcliff swore. The trees were so dense! She already had some people on the ground but she'd need a lot more.

DC Summers had briefed her about Tatiana's disappearing act in the museum cinema – so at least *he* had some kind of excuse; but what about Catterick and Jensen?

Radcliff shook her head. The ultimate responsibility for the girls' safety lay with her, and it was she who had to spearhead the search to track them down.

Smiler was sweating so much it looked like he'd gone swimming in his clothes. He took a slug of water from a polystyrene cup.

'I don't like it,' he muttered, emptying the cup. 'There's two of them, for God's sake. TWO of them.'

'I know that,' snapped back Harding, 'but freaking out won't get us anywhere, will it?'

'So what are we going to do?' demanded Smiler. 'How the hell are we going to find out which one is Tatiana and which one is her doppelgänger?'

Harding caressed the stubble on his chin for a few moments. 'Look, it's fairly obvious what's going on here. One of them is Tatiana and one of them is a body double – a decoy.'

'But they both look exactly the same. I thought a body double was supposed to take the focus *away* from the target.'

Harding sighed. 'You're right, but in this case that hasn't happened.'

'So who is who?'

'I have no idea.'

'So what's the plan?'

Harding thought about this for another minute. 'The way I see it, it doesn't make much difference. We have Tatiana, the other girl is now part of the package and if we play this right we could turn that to our advantage.'

'How?'

'I'm working on it. We stick to the plan, get the cash and get out of the country.'

Smiler nodded anxiously. 'OK,' he muttered.

'It better be,' hissed Harding. 'There's a lot resting on this and I don't want you losing your nerve.'

'I *said* OK,' snapped Smiler.

Harding scowled at him and then checked his mobile phone.

The room smelled of damp wood and decay. A light fitting with a naked, flickering light bulb hung above them. Bits of Blu-tack clung to the walls. Presumably, someone had once worked in this boxroom. What a job that must have been – an office with no natural light.

The girls were silent – each locked in her own world. Venus paced, feeling clammy and uncomfortable in her clothes. The room was warm and muggy and its lack of oxygen bothered her. She started to search the place again for possible escape routes but again she drew a blank. She felt the hammer of panic thudding in her chest. How the hell was she going to get them out of this mess?

Ten minutes went by as she desperately searched for an ingenious method of breaking free. It was maddening. Surely with all her stunt skills, there must be a way. She could try and jump the men when they returned, but this wasn't a big open space like before – this was a tiny enclosed room with a narrow corridor outside; and however agile she was, there were two of them and one had a gun.

And then, about five minutes later, suddenly something struck her. She thought about all of the kidnap stories she'd read in the papers and seen on TV. Sure, some of them wound up in a grisly fashion, but in her memory, didn't most of them end up with a ransom being paid and the hostages being released?

She and Tatiana were hostages, right? Tatiana was a rising film star. Someone somewhere would surely be prepared to fork out a large sum of money to get Tatiana out of here. Maybe this situation wasn't quite as desperate as she thought. Maybe they didn't have to escape. Maybe they just had to sit tight, wait for the ransom money to be paid and after that, the men would let them go. The men had a gun, but this was probably just a deterrent. Yes, in all likelihood the men would get their cash and then bolt. Although every bone in her body shouted for her to find a way to escape, her mind slowly started to relax a bit as the edge was taken off her panic.

However much my instinct is to escape, we sit tight. We sit and wait for the ransom to be paid.

This went against her heart, but her brain insisted on this strategy – at least for the moment.

Her thoughts then turned to Kate's text message. Were Althorp Defence behind this whole thing? And if they were, what was their angle?

Finally Tatiana spoke, her voice was cracked and dry. 'How could this happen?' she asked, with the strain of fear in her eyes.

Venus stopped pacing for a second and stared down at Tatiana. Even though she felt a tiny bit more relaxed, her hostility level towards Tatiana hadn't dropped a millimetre.

'How could it happen?' Venus asked with incredulity. 'It happened because you left the auditorium to make a phone call! It happened because you thought you knew better than the police! It happened because you strut around like you own the place and don't take notice of anyone else!'

All of Venus's anger at Tatiana spilled out in those few sentences. Tatiana stared up at Venus with anguish plastered across her face. She started crying again.

'Give it a rest will you!' snapped Venus furiously.

Tatiana was reduced to choking sobs.

Venus looked away. There was no way she was going to feel any sympathy towards Tatiana. If only the actress hadn't been so stupid and selfish. She'd led them straight into the kidnappers' trap!

Tatiana's sobs gradually dried up and there was silence again in the room. Venus scratched her neck. The hot, stuffy air clung to her body. She felt flushed and stifled. She was staring at the door for the thousandth time when Tatiana mumbled something shakily.

Venus ignored her. She was in no mood to face any more of Tatiana's histrionics.

Tatiana repeated herself, but this time in a much clearer voice. 'Do you think they're going to kill us?' she asked.

Venus wiped a thin line of sweat from her cheek. She sighed heavily and slumped down on to the floor.

'Do you think they will?' asked Tatiana again.

Slowly Venus turned to face Tatiana. The actress had watery smudges of black mascara down both cheeks, her lipstick had extended itself on to her chin, her hair was dry and matted and her pupils were dilated with terror and uncertainty. She looked more like a recycled horror-film puppet than a classy Hollywood actress.

Venus rubbed her temples. Could she be bothered to talk to Tatiana after everything that had gone on this week? The actress had gone out of her way to be unpleasant and undermining; she'd behaved appallingly.

Venus sighed heavily. 'I don't think so,' she muttered. 'I reckon in situations like these, there's a ransom to be paid and the people are usually then freed.'

'Really?' asked Tatiana.

'You're the actress,' snapped Venus, 'you must have seen all those kidnap movies.'

Tatiana wiped her eyes with her hands. 'Could they be terrorists or something?' Tatiana eventually asked.

'I don't think so,' Venus replied. 'I think all we can do is sit tight and wait for the ransom to be handed over.'

'Do you think they've already asked for the ransom?' Tatiana whined.

Venus gritted her teeth. 'Look, Tatiana, I don't know any more than you, do I? I haven't got a clue what's going on. There's no way out of here, so we just sit here until something happens. Have you got a better idea?'

Tatiana shook her head mournfully.

'*Drama queen!*' cursed Venus under her breath.

'Oh,' whispered the actress, looking wounded.

Venus scowled at Tatiana; it was a bit late for the Hollywood teenager to feel any remorse.

When will the damn ransom be paid? And where is DCI Radcliff when you need her?

DCI Radcliff perched on the edge of the table and

pointed to the map and two large photos on the wall. Thirty pairs of eyes were focused intently on her every move.

'OK,' she began, pointing to the photos. 'We are dealing with an abduction of two teenage girls. We're pretty sure that there will be a ransom demand. Both of them are wearing jeans, long-sleeved white T-shirts, sunglasses and trainers. They look very much like each other. One is an American actress called Tatiana Fairfleet – some of you will have heard of her. The other is a girl called Venus Spring – she's been acting as Tatiana's body double for the week. We were watching them, but something went badly wrong in our surveillance operation. I don't want to go into any of that now.'

She indicated the large area of woodland on the map. 'One of our officers spoke to a truck driver who saw a car containing two adult males and two teenage girls entering the woodland. The girls closely match the description of our two. I think it was Tatiana and Venus and I think they're still in that wood.'

Radcliff took a sip of water from her bottle. 'The men are armed. Our officers have identified at least one firearm, but there may be more. I have an armed team down there already, but I don't want to go in heavy-handed until we're completely sure where the girls are being held. I need all of you to join the hunt.'

A female officer coughed. A telephone rang somewhere down the corridor.

'I want you lot in pairs, combing every inch of this area.

This is a very delicate situation, so I've ordered a media blackout. I know this could prevent any potential eye-witnesses coming forward, but although it's a dense wood there can't be that many hiding places down there. I think with enough officers, we'll find them.'

Radcliff took another sip of water.

'Remember,' she said. 'These men are armed and dangerous. I don't want anyone taking any risks. At the first sign of a gun I want you to radio in, and the armed unit will mobilise on my command. If you think you're anywhere near the kidnappers, use your radio immediately. Is everyone clear about that?'

Thirty voices said, 'Yes, ma'am.'

'Good.' Radcliff nodded . 'Now get out there and find them.'

Venus and Tatiana were both still sitting on the floor. Tatiana stared at her trainers. Venus focused on the ceiling.The tension crackled like static electricity in the room. There were streaks of sweat on both girls' faces. The room had become even stuffier and the heat was oppressive and incessant.

Come on, pleaded Venus. *Pay the cash and get us out.*

'Can I just say something,' whispered Tatiana.

Venus shrugged her shoulders non-committally.

'It was great back there when you took them on,' said Tatiana. 'It was really like in a film.'

Venus was taken by surprise. Was this a serious compliment or just another one of Tatiana's bitchy mind games?

Venus stayed tight-lipped.

After a minute or so she let out a grudging response. 'You did OK yourself, I s'pose,' she replied.

'I did nothing,' replied Tatiana miserably.

Venus pondered this statement. It actually wasn't true. Could she be bothered to put it straight?

'You said you were the real Tatiana too.'

'Big deal.'

'No,' replied Venus, suddenly feeling a crumb of empathy with Tatiana. 'You could have kept your mouth shut and let them think it was me.'

'That was the least I could do,' whispered Tatiana.

Venus let this comment go.

'Dennis.'

'Carla?'

'I've got some bad news.'

'Is it Venus?'

'Yes.'

'Oh my God; what's happened to her?'

'It's about her and Tatiana.'

'Don't tell me – they've been kidnapped?'

Radcliff was silent for a few seconds. 'The kidnappers got a lucky break.'

'I don't believe this!' exclaimed Dennis furiously. 'You said the risks were minimal. You said you had people in place.'

'I did have.'

'So what the hell happened?'

'I'm sorry, Dennis; they were caught off guard.'

'Caught off guard!' replied Dennis, burning with anger. 'This is *my granddaughter* we're talking about! I can't believe you let this happen. Do you have any leads?'

'Yes, we're pretty sure she's being kept in woodland, just north of Elstree – where you're working.'

'You have to find her.'

'I know, Dennis. I'm on it.'

'I can't believe it's actually happened,' muttered Dennis. 'What if they kill them or hurt them?'

'I don't think that will happen, Dennis. The intelligence was about a kidnap-for-cash plot – nothing else.'

'OK. Where are you now?'

'I've been in the search helicopter. I'm back at base now.'

'I'll be there in twenty minutes.'

'No, Dennis, I'm not sure if that's a very good idea —'

But Dennis had already slammed down the receiver.

Venus stretched her arms and yawned. They'd been locked up in here for ages without food and drink. Sitting tight was all well and good but Venus didn't know how much more of this disgusting, airless room she could stand. She was developing a terrible headache. She stood up and walked over to the door and started thumping it with her fists.

'We're dying in here!' she shouted. 'We need something to drink!'

A few minutes later, the girls heard the bolts being pulled back and keys turning in the locks. Instinctively, they both stood up.

It was Harding. In one hand he held a plastic bag. In the other he held the gun.

'This is for you two.' He dropped the bag on the floor.

Venus picked it up and looked inside. There were two wrapped cheese and pickle sandwiches and a couple of plastic bottles of Coke.

'About time too,' snapped Venus.

'Shut it!' growled Harding.

'Make me!' shouted Venus, glaring furiously at him. 'When's the ransom gonna be paid and when are you going to let us out of this dump?'

'I said, shut it!' shouted Harding menacingly.

Tatiana quickly placed herself between Venus and Harding. 'Let's just eat this,' Tatiana said quietly.

Venus stared angrily at Harding for a few more seconds and then slumped back down on to the floor.

Harding glowered at Venus in return, backed away and shut the door behind him.

The bolts slid into place and the locks turned shut.

'Not the Savoy Grill, but better than nothing I suppose,' muttered Venus, reaching for one of the sandwiches.

They sat on the floor and devoured the sandwiches before making quick work of the Cokes. The pain in Venus's temples eased off a bit as the girls' blood-sugar returned to acceptable levels.

'Look, Venus, about the way I was in school . . .'

Venus stared at her. 'What about it?'

'I . . . I was a real jerk. I know I was. I don't know why, I guess it's just the whole Hollywood ego-trip getting to me. I've been looking down on everyone else for such a long time that it's become a habit.'

Here we go, thought Venus, *the Hollywood confessional. How phoney can you get?*

'I've behaved pathetically,' went on Tatiana. 'I'm . . . I'm sorry.'

Venus scanned the actress's face. She looked dead serious about this. Venus sighed deeply. 'All right, all right, apology accepted,' she answered testily.

A few more minutes went by.

'Anyway,' said Tatiana, 'how do you know all of that kickboxing stuff? Are you training to be an Olympic champion or something?'

'No,' Venus replied, after a long silence. 'Have you heard of Kelly Tanner?'

'What have we got?' Dennis asked DCI Radcliff, stress written all over his face. His initial anger had switched to panic as the full implications of Venus's kidnap hit home. He'd agreed to the whole Bertram's thing. *He* was responsible for Venus's safety. Why hadn't he just said no? Venus was strong-willed, but she was only fourteen. He shouldn't have let her have a say in the decision – he should have just put his foot down. He and Carla Radcliff went back a very long way, but nothing should cloud his judgement when it came to protecting his granddaughter.

There was also Venus's mum to consider. If Gail found out, his relationship with her would be ruined for ever. He considered the bleak prospect of being cut off by his only daughter. It was too unbearable to take on.

'I'm sure they're being kept in this area here,' explained Radcliff, pointing to the large circle of woodland on the map.

Dennis scowled. 'But it's massive. It could take days to find them.'

Radcliff pursed her lips. 'I know, Dennis – but I've got a big team down there, with some very experienced officers. I'm confident we'll find the girls soon. We've just got to play it safely. If the kidnappers sense we're on to them it might place the girls in more danger.'

Dennis stared at the map as if it would somehow reveal Venus's whereabouts.

'However appalling this whole thing is,' added Radcliff, 'there's one factor we've got to take on board; Venus is a very savvy kid. She'll be OK.'

'You can't know that!' snapped Dennis. 'There's a gun in there. She could have been shot.'

'I know,' Radcliff replied, 'but I'm sure these men are just after money. Tatiana's studio in Hollywood have a four-movie deal with her that's got to be worth millions.'

'What about her parents?'

'They're in the air as we speak. They caught the first available flight.'

'OK,' said Dennis. 'What can I do?'

Carla placed a hand on his shoulder gently. 'Just sit tight, Dennis,' she replied. 'Sit tight and let us find them.'

* * *

'. . . and your granddad is this big-shot stuntman?' asked Tatiana.

'Yeah,' Venus replied. 'He's cool. He's worked with every-one.'

Venus still felt incredibly wary of Tatiana, but the actress did seem genuinely interested in the stunt world. Despite being in three movies, she'd never had much to do with the stunt people.

'And you seriously want to follow him into that kind of work?' asked Tatiana.

'Yeah,' replied Venus. 'The stunt world is pretty small; after a while you get to know most people.'

'Do you need, like, qualifications?'

Venus nodded. 'It's all really regulated. You need to pass loads of tests in things like sword-fighting, escaping from fire, that kind of thing.'

'But aren't you scared you're going to get injured?'

'Of course! But the whole idea is that you make the stunt as safe as possible. Dennis is obsessed with safety checks. It drives me a bit mad sometimes, but I know he's right. There have been some horrific injuries to stunt people who've been slack.'

'But even if you do all your safety checks you can still get hurt, right?'

'Yeah, but I'm not really allowed to do stunts *in films* yet, because I'm fourteen. When a director is absolutely stuck for stunt personnel, they *might* use someone younger, but it's very, very rare.'

'Hang on a second,' blurted out Tatiana in surprise. 'You're only fourteen?'

Venus nodded.

'Unbelievable – you *so* look older.'

'I know,' agreed Venus. 'It can be very useful.'

'You'd never catch me doing one of those stunts,' said Tatiana. 'I'd be too petrified.'

'Well, you'd never catch me acting,' replied Venus, 'I couldn't stand all of the bitchiness among actors.'

'Ah,' said Tatiana sagely. 'You have a point.'

They talked for ages. To Venus's surprise, she gradually found herself really opening up and telling Tatiana things she'd never told anyone other than Kate. She talked about her dad and the way he'd left when she was tiny. She told Tatiana of her yearning to meet him and the feeling she had that she never would. She then told her all about the Jed situation – how she really liked him but was devastated about the cancelled weekend.

In return, Tatiana told Venus about her pushy parents, who had little money but bags of determination for her to succeed as an actress, as well as the way Hollywood worked – the studio chiefs, mad actors and hangers-on.

Eventually they lapsed into silence.

After a while Venus heard soft snores coming from the other side of the room. Tatiana was curled up on the floor with her eyes tightly shut. Venus yawned and realised how tired she was and figured it must be evening. She lay down on the hard floor, rolled up her jacket and stuffed it under her head. She studied the ceiling for a few minutes, until sleep overcame her.

* * *

Venus woke with a crick in her neck. She scrunched her

eyes up for a few seconds as she remembered where she was. She looked across the floor. Tatiana was still asleep.

Venus stood up and stretched her neck – left, then right. It clicked.

The room felt even more airless than before.

A sudden surge of anger rose inside her. She strode over to the door and started hammering on it with her fists.

'OPEN THE DOOR!' she shouted at the top of her voice.

Tatiana sat up. 'What's going on?' she asked through bleary eyes.

'I said OPEN THE DOOR!' yelled Venus.

Footsteps approached, bolts moved and the door slowly opened. Harding stood in the doorway holding the gun.

'We're baking in here!' shouted Venus furiously. 'When are you going to let us go?'

'Shut it!' hissed Harding.

'No, I will *not* shut it,' growled Venus. 'It's bad enough that you're holding us against our will, but you're also denying us basic rights like AIR! If you're caught, we'll tell them that you treated us terribly and they'll double your sentence.'

Harding raised his free hand.

'What?' glared Venus. 'Are you going to hit me? What a tough guy! Striking out at a fourteen-year-old girl!'

Harding's eyes glinted with satisfaction. 'Thanks for that,' he sneered. 'At least we now know that you're not Tatiana, because Tatiana is sixteen, aren't you, Tatiana?'

He glared at Tatiana.

Venus gulped. *What have I done?*

'You're disgusting!' shouted Venus, taking a step towards him and trying to cover up her error. 'The two of you. You're scum!'

She was pushing it and she knew it.

Harding raised the gun towards Venus's forehead.

'Leave her alone!' said Tatiana, quickly stepping over. 'The heat's just getting to us, that's all.'

Harding curled his top lip with contempt and spat on the floor. 'Fine. I'll stay out here and leave this door open for a while,' he muttered angrily.

'I need the loo, too,' said Venus sharply.

Harding pointed the butt of the gun at a door leading to a room next to the one in which they were being kept. Venus stepped out and pushed open the door; it was a toilet – another windowless room. What was it with this building? Had aliens who didn't need oxygen worked here?

When Venus had finished, Tatiana also used the toilet.

When they were both back in the room, Harding kept the door open. He stood against the wall just outside, gun in hand and no expression on his face.

SATURDAY

Dennis Spring sat in an office chair in the police conference room and swore again. He checked his watch. One a.m. When was there going to be some news? The waiting was unbearable. Radcliff had promised him that he could go out with her and join the search, but she hadn't been in contact for ages. Had a ransom demand been received?

He rummaged in his pocket and pulled out the letter he'd recently received. He scanned its contents again. Why did all this have to kick off now? Venus was out there somewhere and he couldn't deal with anything else at present. Venus was his granddaughter. If anything happened to her, he'd never be able to forgive himself; his life would be ruined.

Come on, he urged his mobile phone for the umpteenth time. *Ring me with something positive.*

'Has Saffron Ritchie had a boob job?' asked Tatiana.

Venus managed a grin in response to Tatiana's question. 'Surely *you're* in a better position to know than me.'

'I'm *so* not. I've never seen her in the flesh – but you have, haven't you? Come on, what's the verdict?'

'I don't know,' Venus replied. 'She's always wearing these weird costumes, so it's impossible to tell.'

Tatiana laughed.

Harding was no longer listening in. He'd locked and bolted the door again. 'I'll be back soon,' he'd announced gruffly.

'Dennis has promised to get us tickets for the première of *Airborne Sword*,' said Venus, thinking for a moment about the future, 'but he hasn't managed to yet.'

'Well, he sounds amazingly well connected. If anyone's going to get them, I reckon it will be him.'

'I s'pose you're right,' nodded Venus.

Tatiana flicked a speck of dust out of her eye.

They said nothing for a while.

'Jed really likes you,' said Tatiana suddenly.

Venus stared at her. 'You reckon?'

Tatiana nodded. 'I've been thinking about what you said about him. I reckon he's crazy about you.'

'Really?'

'Definitely,' replied Tatiana with a smile.

'So you don't think the Australian aunt and uncle thing is a smokescreen? Like, maybe to cover for another girlfriend?'

'Are you crazy?' tutted Tatiana. 'Look, I'm not really one to talk about boyfriends with any authority – because the longest relationship I've ever had was with a boy called Danny Kellogg and it only lasted two months – but it sounds as if Jed is completely into you. Don't fret so much about it. Relax and enjoy it. The first available weekend, he'll come running down to London, I'm telling you.'

Venus felt an unexpected wave of calm sweep over her.

Life was mad. Yesterday, if Tatiana Fairfleet had started issuing relationship advice she'd probably have decked her. But now, here, in this airless, stuffy hellhole, it felt good to get her viewpoint.

'Cheers,' she said, nodding at Tatiana. 'Was that boy's surname really Kellogg?'

Tatiana nodded glumly. 'And he *hated* cornflakes.'

There was a second's pause, and then they both burst out laughing.

After the laughter faded, Tatiana's face suddenly clouded over again. 'How long do you think they're going to keep us here?' she asked.

Venus shrugged. 'No idea. But I reckon they'll have put in their ransom demand. They'll probably already have contacted your parents.'

'It won't have been my mom and dad. They couldn't afford it.'

'Well then, maybe the studio you work for?'

Tatiana thought about this. 'Yeah – maybe. I'm signed up with them for a long-term deal, but it depends how much these guys are asking for.'

Venus shrugged her shoulders. In the movies they always asked for ten million dollars and someone had to relay this news to the family or organisation who was expected to pay.

But this wasn't the movies. Maybe others were involved.

All we have to go on at the moment is the two creeps out there. How much will they ask for? Impossible to tell.

'I'm bored,' Tatiana suddenly announced, after a silence of about fifteen minutes.

'Me too,' replied Venus.

'Shall we ask for a TV?'

Venus laughed.

'How about a DVD player?'

Venus laughed again.

Tatiana sighed heavily.

'Hang on a sec,' said Venus. She pulled at the elastic tying her hair back. 'I bet you can't get this to land directly on to that nail on top of the desk over there,' she said.

'Bet I can.'

'Go on then.'

Venus handed the elastic to Tatiana.

Tatiana stretched it in her hand, held it up and threw it forward. It hit the corner of the desk and fell to the floor.

'That was terrible,' she laughed. 'Your turn.'

Venus retrieved the elastic from the floor. She sat back down on the floor next to Tatiana and lobbed it forward. It landed on top of the desk, but well away from the nail.

Harding put the phone down.

'Well?' demanded Smiler anxiously.

'Bad news,' replied Harding. 'The studio are stalling us. They're going on about how they have to get the payment authorised.'

'No way!' said Smiler, twitchily. 'We were told it would be totally smooth.'

Harding was lost in thought for a few seconds. 'Right,' he suddenly announced. 'We know which one is Tatiana now, so this is what we're going to do. If the payment isn't authorised in the next ten minutes, we kill the other girl.'

Smiler stood up shakily. 'You can't be serious?'

'Of course I'm serious,' Harding replied. 'We haven't got time for messing about. We need to show them we mean business. If they refuse to pay, the other girl gets it. You watch how quickly they'll move after that. Then we keep Tatiana with us until we've got the cash and are well away, release her and disappear.'

'I don't know,' said Smiler, biting his nails frantically.

Harding scowled at him. 'Ten minutes or the kickboxer girl dies.'

Smiler rubbed his hands together nervously.

Harding picked up the phone again and started dialling.

Venus flipped the hair band forward again. They'd each had ten goes, but neither of them had got it on to the nail. It was infuriating but somehow addictive.

The hair elastic skimmed over the desk's surface and disappeared down the back of it.

'That's rubbish,' Venus groaned. 'But I'm not giving up till I do it.'

Venus stood up slowly, walked over to the desk and leaned right over it. She saw that half of the elastic was sticking up from a groove between two floorboards, behind the desk.

'Have you got it?' asked Tatiana.

'It's stuck,' replied Venus. She got down on all fours and crawled under the desk to retrieve the elastic, but it wouldn't budge. She grabbed hold and put her weight into it. Suddenly, it came free, causing Venus to fall against the wall next to the desk.

An echoey sound rang out.

Harding stood in the corridor staring at his watch. Seven minutes were up. The phone hadn't rung.

'Right,' snapped Harding.

Smiler stared at him with horror.

'I've had enough of this,' growled Harding.

'They've got three more minutes,' pointed out Smiler, his body shaking with anxiety.

'I know, but I'm heading back there now.'

Harding strode towards the room where the girls were being held. He'd made his call and set down his terms. They hadn't got back to him. He'd have to shoot the kickboxer. The time passed quickly and his hand was just reaching out for the top bolt, when Smiler sped down the corridor, waving the phone at him.

'It's them,' hissed Smiler. 'They say they need another ten minutes.'

Harding grabbed the phone.

'Hey, Venus, get over here! They're outside. I can hear them. Harding's on the phone.'

Venus got up, looking thoughtfully at the wall, and

hurried across the room. The girls squashed their ears against the door and listened.

'Right,' Harding hissed furiously into the phone. 'You've got ten more minutes, but that's it. If that payment is not authorised by the time those ten minutes are up, the other girl dies.'

Smiler gulped anxiously and followed Harding, who was already storming angrily back down the corridor.

On the other side of the door, Venus and Tatiana looked at each other in horror. They'd heard every word.

'Oh my God!' said Tatiana in a trembling voice. 'They're going to *kill* you!'

Venus's whole body was gripped by fear. Ten minutes! Harding was clearly a ruthless criminal, he probably wouldn't blink an eyelid before shooting her. The idea of sitting tight was not an option any more. They had to get out. Her life was now on the line.

Tatiana was shaking with fear.

'Keep it together,' hissed Venus.

Venus's mind was fizzing with terror. She looked round the room again for the millionth time. OK, there was no way to escape; she'd have to take the men on. She'd have to get the gun and somehow get them out of here. She'd need Tatiana's help as well. *But what if . . . ?*

'W . . . w . . . what are we going to do?' stuttered Tatiana.

Venus crossed the room and pounded the wall by the desk again, harder this time. The echoey sound filled the room. *Definitely hollow . . .*

Harding and Smiler sat in the kitchen. Smiler checked his watch nervously. 'They've had three minutes,' he said.

Both men stared at the silent phone.

Harding held the gun even tighter. He felt the resolve inside him like a steel tube. He was a man of his word.

'What the hell are you doing?' moaned Tatiana. 'I reckon we've only got about six minutes left.'

'It's hollow,' whispered Venus.

'What's hollow?' asked Tatiana as she hurried across the room and crouched down by the desk.

'There must be an open space behind the wall,' muttered Venus. 'It must be some kind of disused shaft, or something.'

'Are you serious?' whispered Tatiana.

Venus nodded.

'Well, hit the damn thing again,' pleaded Tatiana.

Venus hit it again and her fist made a tiny dent in the wall and a few flakes of plaster crumbled down on to the floor.

'Pass my jacket,' Venus commanded.

Tatiana rushed across the room and brought it over to her. Venus wrapped her jacket round her fist and lashed out again at the wall. This time a big chunk of plaster cascaded down.

'Hurry up,' urged Tatiana.

Two more punches and a fist-sized hole had appeared. Venus adjusted her position and this time used her right foot. She kicked as hard as she could and a huge chunk of plaster was ripped out and thrown backwards into the hole.

'And another one,' said Tatiana, stretching her foot out and kicking the wall herself.

Three kicks later, they had created a hole that was just about big enough for Venus to squeeze her head through. She peered upwards.

'What's in there?' hissed Tatiana.

'There's moonlight at the top!' Venus whispered. 'It *is* a shaft.'

She pulled her head back out, turned her body round and kicked violently at the wall. Several chunks of plaster came away.

'We've got to hurry,' pleaded Tatiana, helping to kick the plaster away.

It took eight more kicks and they'd made a hole that they could both fit through.

'Give me an update,' demanded DCI Radcliff into the phone. She listened intently, looking up from a table next to the large map in the briefing room, with Dennis at her side.

'Progress is slow, ma'am,' reported a junior officer. 'It's a big area and there are thousands of possible hiding places. I'm not saying it's a needle in a haystack, but it's tough.'

'Well keep at it!' snapped Radcliff. 'And keep me posted all the time.'

Radcliff ended the call and looked up at Dennis.

His forehead was crinkled with deep grooves of worry.

'We'll get them, Dennis. I guarantee you we'll get them.'

Dennis looked at Radcliff anxiously. He didn't share her optimism. In fact, he was starting to fear the worst.

Harding glanced down at his watch. The phone had remained silent. He'd warned them . . . so they couldn't say they hadn't known the score.

Four minutes till shooting time.

The shaft was narrow and full of dust and cobwebs. Grime was caked on its walls. Thankfully, it wasn't a perfectly formed structure, so there were enough chunks of bricks sticking out to act as footholds.

Venus made quick progress. The pull-ups she'd recently started doing were paying dividends. Her forearms were strong and she made it to the top easily.

Tatiana, on the other hand, was struggling.

'I don't think I can make it,' she hissed up nervously.

'You can!' whispered Venus. 'Just take it nice and steady.'

'I'm not sure . . .'

Venus lowered herself down towards Tatiana. 'Grab hold of my leg,' she instructed. She went a bit lower and Tatiana caught hold of her right leg.

'OK,' said Venus, edging back up. The climb was far harder with another human being to carry, but Venus gritted her teeth and kept focused, while Tatiana did her best to help by finding footholds.

'You're doing well, Tatiana,' Venus whispered encouragingly. 'Just keep on climbing.'

When Venus reached the top she looked down into the dim light at Tatiana. 'OK, we're here. Let go of me and grab on to that brick there.'

Anxiously Tatiana did as she was told.

Venus pushed herself backwards out of the square opening. She perched on the edge of the shaft and reached her hand down for Tatiana. Tatiana grabbed it and pulled herself up next to Venus.

From this lofty position they saw that they were on the roof of a building in a vast, sprawling industrial park. The place was dark, deserted and eerie. Calling for help would probably prove fruitless and could get them caught again.

'That's our way down,' said Venus, pointing to the top of a narrow fire escape that clung to the side of the building.

Venus swung her legs over the edge of the roof and jumped down on to the narrow ledge below. A quivering Tatiana followed her.

'This way,' beckoned Venus.

They crept along the ledge and stepped over a line of steel pipes. Venus eased herself over the railings of the fire escape and helped Tatiana do the same. They were now on the fire escape itself – a small platform three flights up. They took a few exploratory steps. Suddenly Venus pressed herself against the wall and motioned for Tatiana to do the same. Venus pointed to an open window.

'They're in there,' she mouthed silently.

She signalled for Tatiana to get down and move forwards. Silently Tatiana got on to her hands and knees and crawled fearfully underneath the windowsill.

She stood up only once she was well past it.

Venus followed suit but when she was halfway across, she raised her head a few millimetres.

Tatiana shook her hand violently but Venus took a quick peep through the window. Harding and Smiler were sitting at an oval table with their backs to her. 'Right,' announced Harding. 'They've got two minutes left.'

Venus gulped with fear, but at that second she spotted a low table, just next to the window. On the top of the table was a bunch of keys. One of them had a BMW logo.

Tatiana was madly gesticulating for Venus to stop what she was doing, but Venus realised immediately that a successful escape could depend on what she did in the next few seconds.

Agonisingly slowly, she reached her hand through the open window.

Smiler coughed.

Venus withdrew her hand and ducked as Smiler stood up, walked in her direction and grabbed a bottle of water that was sitting on top of a filing cabinet. If heartbeats could be heard outside the body, Venus's would've sounded like a symphony orchestra.

She held her breath and waited thirty seconds before raising her head again. To her relief, Smiler had returned to his chair by the oval table.

Venus reached her hand through the open window again. She stretched forward and clenched her fist round the bunch of keys. Lifting them into the air incredibly slowly and carefully, she drew the keys towards her.

Tatiana was completely freaking out but Venus carried on with her task. Delicately, she moved the keys out past the window frame.

'One minute,' she heard Harding hiss.

Oh my God. One minute!

She ducked back down and started crawling again, the keys safely in her hand.

Tatiana's face was a mixture of disbelief and admiration.

Venus pointed down the fire escape ladder and put a finger over her lips.

'That's it,' announced Harding. 'Time's up.'

He grasped the gun and left the room.

Venus and Tatiana really started moving now. They got down the first flight in less than ten seconds.

Smiler lit a couple of matches and let them burn right down until they nearly scorched his fingers. In a few seconds the girl would be dead. Harding could shoot people – he, Smiler, never had the stomach for it. He was about to light another match, when he heard the earth-shaking roar of Harding's voice.

'They've gone!'

For Smiler it was as if his whole world was suddenly a slow-motion movie and filmed through a hazy yellow filter. As his mind processed what Harding had yelled, he got up out of his chair and lunged for the car keys on the table next to the window.

'Where are the keys?' yelled Smiler. 'I left them on the table!'

'You must have moved them!' said Harding, bursting into the room.

'I d . . . d . . . didn't,' stammered Smiler.

'Listen!' commanded Harding.

A faint metallic clanging rang out.

'They're on the fire escape!' Harding yelled.

Smiler threw himself out of the window on to the fire escape. He instantly saw the girls two flights down.

Harding tumbled out after him.

'Get them!' he barked.

Venus and Tatiana were at the top of the final flight of stairs when they heard shouts from above. Harding and Smiler were tearing down the fire escape ladders – they were both ashen-faced and wore expressions of desperation.

Venus's feet smacked on to the ground at the bottom of the last ladder. She pulled Tatiana down the last few steps.

'Which way?' screamed Tatiana.

Venus's mind was working furiously. She had a pretty good idea which way to go. She sprinted off to the right, with Tatiana right behind her. They pushed open a door that led back inside and ran along a deserted corridor.

It was a dead-end.

To their right were two further doors. Instantly Venus kicked open the left one. It was a store cupboard.

She kicked the right one. It opened out into a dimly lit but empty garage. Parked at its centre was the BMW.

'Get them!' yelled Harding, close behind them.

Venus clicked the remote button on the car key and the

central locking system opened all of the car doors. Venus leaped into the driver's seat. Tatiana tumbled in on the passenger side.

'Shut your door!' screamed Venus.

Tatiana yanked her door shut and Venus pushed her lock down – locking all of the other doors at the same time.

A second later, Smiler appeared at Venus's window.

Her body jolted in shock.

Smiler grabbed the door handle and started pulling wildly at it.

'What are we going to do?' shrieked Tatiana. 'You can't drive – can you?'

Venus stuffed the key into the ignition.

'Oh my God, you can!' breathed Tatiana in stunned surprise. 'I don't believe it!'

The car spluttered to life.

'Dennis taught me!' shouted Venus. He'd taught her driving at high speeds, swerving, braking and driving off ramps for car jumps. When her mum had once mentioned how good it would be for Venus to have driving lessons when she was seventeen, Venus had to stop herself from laughing. She'd been on tracks and paths that no standard driving instructor would ever use.

Suddenly Harding appeared beside Tatiana's window. He was holding the gun.

'He's going to smash the glass!' yelled Tatiana.

Harding raised the gun in the air but as he brought it crashing towards the passenger window, Venus slammed down the car's accelerator pedal. The tyres hissed violently as the car shot backwards. Harding fell forwards into the empty space vacated by the disappearing car. Smiler jumped out of the vehicle's way to avoid his feet getting crushed by the reversing wheels.

The car hurtled back against the garage door, smashing it open and taking a great metal chunk out of it.

Venus wildly reversed the BMW down the short ramp outside, glancing over her shoulder the whole way.

Thank God for Dennis.

Harding and Smiler were back on their feet and sprinting after the car, shouting and swearing.

'Put your seatbelt on!' yelled Venus, reaching for hers.

The BMW thudded backwards towards the end of a narrow pathway.

Venus yanked the wheel down hard and the car spun one hundred and eighty degrees.

Harding and Smiler were nearly on to them again. Harding had his hand on the rear bumper; Smiler ran forward – he was going to leap on to the boot. But Venus had other plans. She changed gear, floored the accelerator and the BMW shot forward. Smiler was mid-leap. He fell head first on to Harding and both men tumbled to the ground.

'Oh my God!' screamed Tatiana, half laughing, half crying.

The BMW was now hurtling along a narrow road, flanked on either side by large warehouse units.

'We've done it!' shouted Tatiana. 'Drive and let's find a phone box. Then we can call the police!'

Venus's spirits soared too as she sped down the road,

but their moment of elation was short-lived.

There, at the end of the pathway, was a black Mercedes. It was parked across the road and Harding and Smiler were standing in front of it. Harding was clenching the gun.

'How the hell . . . ?' gasped Venus.

Tatiana's face dropped in horror. 'No!' she screamed. 'No! No! No!'

Venus's brain went into overdrive. *Harding and Smiler must have known a shortcut.*

'Turn back!' shrieked Tatiana.

But the BMW was going too fast. Even if she braked violently, they would only pull up short of the Merc if they were lucky. If not, they'd smash straight into it. Multiple deaths were likely.

That was when Venus noticed the skip.

It was jutting out at the side of one of the units on the right. Two thick planks of wood were leading up to it, to enable workmen to tip wheelbarrows of rubbish inside.

It was a long shot – a very long shot – but there was no other option. She had to go for it.

Harding raised the gun.

Venus accelerated.

'What are you doing?' yelled Tatiana. 'You're going to get us killed!'

But Venus ignored Tatiana.

Harding was aiming the gun very carefully. He was pointing it directly at the BMW's front left tyre.

'He's going to blow out the tyre!' shouted Tatiana. 'You have to STOP!'

One of the stunt-driving tests Venus had seen involved taking a car down the narrowest of winding country lanes at speeds of up to a hundred miles an hour. She needed to drive in that spirit now. And she was determined to get herself and Tatiana out of this mess . . . alive.

She pushed her foot harder against the accelerator. If it could have gone down any further, it would have pushed through the car's floor.

Venus saw Harding curling his finger round the trigger. As he pulled it, Venus turned the car violently to the right. A bullet hurtled towards the car's left front tyre but it missed by the tiniest of fractions as the BMW swerved out of its path.

Venus steered the car straight up the two wooden planks leading to the skip. The tyres were perfectly aligned and thankfully, although the planks buckled, they were tough enough not to snap.

'Venus!' screeched Tatiana.

Harding and Smiler gazed in shock as the car flew up the lengths of wood.

As the BMW reached the top of the planks, instead of toppling into the skip, it took off and flew through the air – over Harding and Smiler, who could do nothing but watch its flight with astonishment and horror.

The BMW came crashing down on to the ground several metres behind the Merc – with an incredible smash.

Venus and Tatiana were thrown violently forward in their seats – their seatbelts saving them from horrific injuries. The steering wheel spun crazily and Venus had to use all of her strength to bring it under control, as the hiss of another bullet pierced the air.

Venus frantically pulled the BMW to the left and the bullet hurtled beneath the car, missing the right back tyre by a few centimetres.

In the mirror, Venus saw the men both dive back into the Merc.

Venus caught their expressions; they did not look happy.

Smiler was in the driver's seat and the Merc kicked forward.

Venus steered the BMW forward and five seconds later it was coming to the end of the road. It was a T-junction.

'Which way?' screamed Tatiana, looking back. 'Come on, Venus, they're catching us!'

Venus thought desperately.

'They're nearly on us!' shrieked Tatiana.

Venus saw Harding leaning out of the Merc's passenger window, gun in hand. She pulled the wheel down and the BMW lurched right. Venus stamped on the accelerator again.

A bullet whistled past the car, scraping the front bumper.

The Merc turned right three seconds later.

Venus and Tatiana found themselves on a narrow, winding country road.

'Speed up, Venus – we're bound to come to a main road soon! There'll be people there. Maybe the police will be nearby, looking for us.'

They hurtled towards a crossroads. Venus didn't slow down. She headed straight across it, narrowly avoiding being crushed to pieces by a huge, hooting juggernaut.

'Venus!' screamed Tatiana, putting her hands over her eyes.

'Sorry!' yelled Venus.

'Where are they?' hissed Tatiana, looking over her shoulder.

'There!' replied Venus, looking anxiously in the rear-view mirror.

The Merc had lost a few metres to wait for the juggernaut to pass, but was soon gaining on them again.

They were now on another country road, but this one was slightly wider than the last. They passed a large, darkened building on the right. *Silas Sewage Treatment,* a large grey sign read.

'I don't believe it,' muttered Venus.

'What?' demanded Tatiana.

'I know where we are!'

'What?'

'I've been here before.'

'What are you on about?'

'I've passed that sewage place before. And I know the place they kept us in – I've realised where it is. It's part of this massive industrial estate. Dennis once filmed some rooftop fights there. It's near Elstree Studios.'

Tatiana looked staggered. 'You're not serious!'

'I am,' Venus replied, her eyes on the road as the BMW sped down the lane. 'The studios are only a couple of miles away.'

'But that still doesn't solve the problem of having a gunman on our tail!' pointed out Tatiana.

This was true, but Venus's mind was still feverishly working out her course of action. She jerked her head back and saw Harding aiming the gun at the BMW's tyres again.

She jammed the wheel from side to side, zigzagging on the country road to make it much more difficult for Harding to get a clear shot.

Trees and bushes sped by in snatches of dark greens and browns as the headlights streaked down the road.

Venus's thoughts were moving at a thousand miles an hour. Her hands were clutching the wheel so tightly she felt they might actually disconnect from the rest of her body.

And then she remembered something that Harding had said to Smiler when they were in the garage after arriving at the old warehouse. 'Leave the spare one in there.'

'Check the glove compartment!' Venus commanded Tatiana.

'What for?' asked Tatiana.

'Just chuck it all out,' Venus shouted, checking the rear-view mirror again.

Harding was still trying to get a clear shot in. Another bullet was released.

As Venus dragged the car to the left it missed the wheels, but took out the BMW's back bumper, which clattered backwards on to the road.

Tatiana was throwing things out of the glove compartment at a mad pace. Out of it spilled a London *A–Z*, some driving gloves, two packs of chewing gum, an empty pack of crisps, a road map of the UK and a screwdriver.

'That's all there is!' shouted Tatiana.

But Venus glanced across quickly and noticed a tiny, shiny black surface.

'What's that black thing?' she screamed.

Tatiana reached for it.

The blinding headlights of the Merc were getting nearer by the second.

Venus swore.

Tatiana yanked the black object out. It was a slim mobile phone; the men's spare one.

'Oh my God!' breathed Tatiana.

Venus grabbed it from Tatiana's hand. She kept her right hand on the steering wheel and clutched the mobile with her left. *Please let it work,* prayed Venus.

She pressed the power switch.

Nothing happened.

Tatiana looked from the phone to Venus and back again.

Venus clenched the phone tighter. *Come on! Come on!*

Nothing.

Please!

Suddenly the screen lit up. There was a single bar of power and the reception was very low too, but Venus wasn't waiting around for a more advantageous location. She started punching in a number and was one digit from the end when there was a deafening roar.

A bullet had smashed right through the back window of the BMW. Glass shattered everywhere.

Tatiana and Venus both screamed and instinctively covered their faces.

The BMW skidded across the road.

In the couple of seconds that Venus's eyes were shut, she was certain that death was imminent. But the bullet had hurtled right through the middle of the car, between the girls and crashed through the front windscreen, sending a million more shards of glass on to the bonnet.

They were incredibly lucky not to die.

As the glass rained down on Venus she tried desperately to regain control of the steering wheel, but the car was exercising its own choices now. The BMW mounted a grass verge on the right of the lane, and a huge tree loomed over them. Venus was just able to pull the wheel left and the car missed the tree by centimetres and bounced back on to the road.

Tatiana's eyes were closed and she was still screaming.

Venus stared at the tiny cubes of glass all over her clothes and hair, all over Tatiana and all over the inside of the car – on the dashboard, strewn over the floor. The cold night air rushed in the empty front windscreen and out of the back.

Venus looked round, fragments of glass cascading from her hair in all directions. In the aftershock of the smashed windscreens, the Merc had closed in on them. It was now only a couple of metres behind the BMW. And it was moving in for the kill.

The Merc spurted forwards and smashed into the back of the BMW, forcing it to jolt forward.

'They're coming again!' screamed Tatiana.

The Merc pressed forward again, this time smashing the

girls' car with more force. Venus was still desperate to tap in the last digit on the mobile.

She saw another bend approaching and took it at ferocious speed; one hand on the wheel, the other clutching the mobile. The BMW hurtled round the bend. There was sharp drop to the left and the BMW skidded along the ridge, almost plunging down the side. But Venus managed to keep the car steady. As soon as she was round the bend, she tapped the last digit into the mobile and hit the connect button.

It rang once and a voice answered.

'You've only got one bullet left!' screamed Smiler, his face dripping with sweat, his clammy fingers digging into the steering wheel.

'Get in on them again!' commanded Harding.

'I'm trying,' snapped Smiler in panic, 'but there are buildings up ahead! We'll have to pull out.'

Harding gripped Smiler by the collar. 'Just shut up and drive!' he yelled.

Smiler tugged his shirt free from Harding's grasp and pressed down on the accelerator. A few minutes later, the Merc loomed over the BMW once more.

'One more contact and we'll knock the BMW off the road,' shouted Harding. 'Then we grab the girls and get the hell out of here.'

But without any warning the BMW suddenly spun to the left and crashed into a short cobbled street lined with trees. There was some sort of building at the end of the street but behind it was a high, solid brick wall.

It was a dead-end.

The BMW bounced over the cobbles and screeched to a stop – smoke billowing out of its bonnet.

Smiler slammed on the Merc's brakes and managed to stop it a few metres behind the BMW.

Harding breathed a huge sigh of relief.

'Got 'em,' he snarled, his upper lip curling in determination. 'Let's make this a very quick changeover. And at the next place, we'll stay in the room with them. I'm not being outwitted by two teenage girls again.'

Smiler nodded nervously.

'This is the end of the road for them,' hissed Harding. 'Now let's get this over with and no more screw-ups.'

Harding and Smiler exited the Merc quickly.

'Get out of the car!' Harding commanded in a steely voice, brandishing his gun in the air and taking a step forward. 'Nice and slowly; and you won't get hurt.'

There was no movement from the BMW.

'Get out!' barked Harding again.

Smiler stepped to his side to try and get a better viewpoint. Both girls were in there, sitting up and covered in glass shrapnel.

'I said, get out!' Harding shouted. 'This is where it ends. There's nowhere for you to go.'

Very slowly, Venus and Tatiana emerged from the battered BMW, their backs towards their abductors.

Harding took another step forward. 'That's it,' he said. 'Walk away from the car now.'

Venus and Tatiana started to back towards the men.

'Turn round!' Harding commanded.

The girls turned round.

The kidnappers immediately noticed two things about the girls' expressions. Their faces were white with exhaustion and the frenzy of the chase. But there was something else. In spite of everything, the girls didn't look *scared*.

They'd both seemed pretty terrified back at the industrial park, but now there was a sort of serene calm in their faces. To Harding and Smiler this defied logic. These two girls had been shot at, rammed and chased into this quiet, dead-end road, and yet they looked like *they* were the ones who were in control of this situation.

Smiler glanced nervously at Harding – who for once didn't have his usual look of steely-eyed confidence and power on his face. This made Smiler even more edgy.

Something was wrong – he could feel it.

'OK?' asked Venus, quietly.

Tatiana nodded.

'Let's go for it,' Venus whispered.

They started walking towards Harding and Smiler at an incredibly slow pace.

'Hurry up!' barked Harding impatiently, the gun in his hand.

The girls suddenly stopped and stared at the men.

'Get on with it!' shouted Harding, his voice faltering slightly suspiciously. 'Get into the Merc.'

Venus stared at Smiler and a thin smile appeared on her lips.

At that second there was a loud metallic clang and white lights flooded the street. Harding, Smiler, Venus and Tatiana covered their eyes as the light momentarily blinded them.

'What the —' started Harding, but he didn't get a chance to finish his sentence.

The lights dipped as suddenly as they'd come on and immediately a series of dark shapes appeared in every direction around them. These silhouettes were rooted to their spots and at first, after that blinding flash of light, it was impossible to see what they were. But within seconds, it became very clear. They were people. And they weren't just any people. Every single one was an armed police officer and they were all training their guns directly at Harding and Smiler.

They were on the rooftop of the street's only building, emerging from behind trees and appearing from on top of the brick wall at the end of the street.

A loud, clear, female voice cut through the night.

'This is the police!' she announced. 'You are totally surrounded. Drop the weapon and lie face down on the ground.'

Harding and Smiler stood still in absolute shock.

Neither of them could believe this was happening.

What had gone wrong with the 'straight kidnap' they'd been selected for? How on earth could an armed response unit be here? It was impossible.

For a second, Venus detected a glint of resolve in Harding's eyes, but it was quickly diminished as he took in the scene before him. Suddenly it wasn't the girls who had nowhere to run to – it was he and Smiler. They'd both done time in prison but those sentences would pale into insignificance compared to what they'd get for this crime.

Harding dropped his gun on to the ground. It clattered on the cobbles.

Smiler looked at him in horror. Slowly and laboriously they knelt on the ground and then spread themselves out, face down.

Six officers hurried forward – their guns aimed continuously at the prostrate villains. Harding and Smiler's hands were pulled behind their backs and handcuffed. They were then hauled to their feet and taken away towards a police van.

Just before they were pushed inside, Harding turned round and looked at the girls. Venus thought he seemed to have aged twenty years in the last few minutes and instead of a conspiring and tough criminal, he now looked like a broken man.

Two officers pushed the kidnappers inside the cage at the back of the van, crashed shut the grill, locked it and then slammed the van's back door.

Five seconds later, the van started up and drove towards the end of the street. Moments after that, it was out of sight.

Venus breathed an enormous sigh of relief.

Tatiana stared in wonderment at Venus. 'You're . . . you're unbelievable,' she cried, wrapping her arms round Venus.

Venus looked across at the building at the end of the street. *Lucky Break,* its sign said.

DCI Carla Radcliff emerged from the shadows. She stopped about a metre away from the girls.

'I don't quite know what to say,' she began.

Tatiana released Venus.

'I suppose I better start with well done,' continued the DCI. 'It was a smart move to lure them into this road – a dead-end is always a perfect setting for a sting like this.'

Venus nodded in acknowledgement and then saw another familiar figure walking towards them.

'Granddad!' she shouted and ran over to him.

He gave her an enormous bear hug and kissed her on the forehead. He looked terrible and Venus suddenly felt an aching twinge of guilt. She'd been so wrapped up in getting herself and Tatiana away from Harding and Smiler that she'd hardly given Dennis a thought. He must have been through hell.

The purr of Radcliff's car hummed in the darkness as the DCI drove Venus and Tatiana back to Bertram's. Tatiana had fallen asleep immediately, but Venus was very awake and very alert. Her mind was spinning with a million unanswered questions and puzzles.

'Was Althorp Defence linked to what happened?' Venus asked keenly, staring forward into the folds of the night, where the odd star flickered steadily.

Radcliff shook her head. 'No. I had the place turned over. There was nothing. No connection whatsoever.'

Venus was quiet for a few seconds, deep in thought.

'What about the leak?' she asked. 'Who tipped Harding

and Smiler off about the museum? Was it Mr Foster? He's been acting weirdly all week and I heard him talking about Friday on the phone – he said something was going to happen on Friday. That's got to be dodgy. Plus, any time I've been anywhere near him he's accused me of spying on him.'

Radcliff nodded thoughtfully. 'He left the school site this morning saying he was going to get materials for repairing the tennis-court fence, but this turned out to be a lie.'

'So it *was* him who tipped them off?'

Radcliff shook her head. 'It turns out that Mr Foster has a girlfriend – and therein lies his alibi. He's been able to keep the whole thing secret from Mrs Finch, as he usually visits his lady friend on the weekends. But apparently they had some sort of tiff, and she demanded that he take time off school on Friday and spend the day with her. Rather than face talking about any of this with the headmistress, he made up an excuse. Looks like they needed to do quite a bit of sorting out, because he's still with her. Though, why he feels unable to tell Mrs Finch he's got a girlfriend is anyone's guess.'

Venus pondered this. 'So if it wasn't Foster, it has to be the coach driver,' Venus concluded. 'He was told the destination of the trip when he arrived at the school. It would have been easy to then text this info to Harding and Smiler.'

'That's what I thought,' agreed Radcliff. 'But we searched him and the coach and the only text messages his network found were to his wife and a hardware store. So he might be a DIY bore, but it puts him out of the kidnap picture.'

'Right,' said Venus. 'So who was it?'

'Unfortunately,' said the DCI, 'I don't know yet.'

Twenty minutes later, the DCI pulled her car through the open gates of Bertram's College. Mrs Finch, Miss Sutton and DC Summers were waiting on the carriage drive.

DC Summers walked up to the car and opened the driver's door. 'Ma'am,' he said, nodding to Radcliff.

Venus climbed out. She instantly saw the toll that the kidnap had taken on her form tutor and the headmistress. Their skin looked translucent, their features pinched with worry. Having two girls kidnapped isn't the kind of thing you'd want to put in your school prospectus.

Radcliff leaned back in the car and patted Tatiana on the shoulder. 'We're back at Bertram's,' she said softly.

Tatiana stirred, stretched her arms and sat up slowly. 'What's happening?' she mumbled, easing her way out of the back seat.

'Thank goodness you're both all right,' said Mrs Finch, stepping forward and smiling wearily at the girls.

'We've all been worried sick,' added Miss Sutton. 'Are you two OK?'

Venus nodded, suddenly too tired to speak.

Tatiana pulled a piece of glass out of her hair.

'They're very shaken up,' said Radcliff, 'but they've handled this whole thing superbly. I need to debrief all of you and then it's straight to bed for the girls. As it's Saturday today, I'm assuming they can have a very untaxing day.'

Miss Sutton nodded earnestly. 'I'll see to that,' she replied.

'Good,' said Radcliff. 'Now I want all of you to come inside with me.'

Mrs Finch gravely led the party through the front doors of the school. She took them along a wide corridor, through a large set of double doors into the Great Hall. The headmistress strode across the hall to a door at the far side, which led directly into her study. Venus was lost in thought as she walked with the others and was so busy trying to figure things out that she didn't see the pile of equipment stacked on the newly polished hall floor. She barged straight into it, banging her shins in the process.

Venus winced and looked down. She'd collided into a stack of silver flight cases, neatly resting on top of each other. She was about to move on and return to her brooding, when a flash of recognition suddenly ignited in her brain. Suddenly, she felt wide awake and full of energy again.

Mrs Finch and DC Summers had already disappeared through the headmistress's study door. Tatiana was right behind them and soon she joined them.

Venus didn't move, but it wasn't on account of her bruised shins.

'Miss Sutton,' she called.

The form tutor stopped and turned round. 'Yes, Venus?' she asked.

'You see these cases on the floor – what are they?'

Miss Sutton walked back over to where Venus and the DCI were standing. 'They belong to the school photographer,' Miss Sutton answered. 'Why?'

A bell of sudden clarity clanged inside Venus's head.

'DCI Radcliff,' she said, 'can I have a word with you?'

'Of course,' replied Radcliff. 'You go on ahead, Miss Sutton. We'll catch up with you in a minute.'

Miss Sutton nodded and walked back to the study door and joined the others inside.

Venus waited until the door was fully shut before she spoke. The pieces were rapidly clicking into place for her now. She'd finally realised what this thing was all about.

'Are you all right, Venus?' asked the DCI.

Venus nodded her head slowly. 'There's something I need to tell you,' she replied.

The doorbell rang. Dennis waited a few seconds before he went to open it. He was anxious about this visitor, but the events of the last few hours had put things in better perspective.

He composed himself for a moment and went to open the front door.

'Right,' DCI Radcliff began.

She and Venus had kept everyone waiting in Mrs Finch's study while Venus had disclosed her breakthrough and the DCI had made some calls to bring it all together.

Now Radcliff, Venus, Tatiana, Mrs Finch, Miss Sutton and DC Summers were all in Mrs Finch's office.

'The *good* news, of course, is that Venus and Tatiana are safe,' Radcliff continued. 'We also have the kidnappers in custody. They'll be charged with abduction and extorting money. They won't be granted bail, so they'll be in prison until their trial.'

'Thank heavens for that,' said Miss Sutton.

'My thoughts exactly,' said Radcliff. 'However, there are certain issues that I'd like to resolve.'

No one spoke.

'My starting point,' went on Radcliff, 'is the question of how these men knew that Miss Sutton's tutor group were going to visit the museum. DC Summers has confirmed that the coach wasn't followed, so the kidnappers were already in place, waiting for the girls. Someone tipped them off – someone on the inside – but who?'

Miss Sutton coughed anxiously.

'Aside from the officers I assigned to the case,' explained Radcliff, 'the only people who knew in advance where that coach was heading were Mrs Finch, Miss Sutton and Mr Foster. The coach driver was informed on arrival at the school.'

The tension gripped everyone in the room with its curling, jittery fingers.

'I have ruled out the coach driver and Mr Foster from my enquiries,' announced the DCI. 'Neither of them tipped off the kidnappers; neither of them is involved.'

'I . . . I don't understand,' said Miss Sutton.

'I have also ruled *you* out, Miss Sutton. Having spoken to DC Summers I am certain that you weren't involved either.'

There was absolute silence in the room following this announcement. All eyes turned to face Mrs Finch. She shrank back defensively. 'Surely you're not implying that *I* was —'

Radcliff cut her short. 'I'm going to let Venus pick up the story,' said the DCI.

Mrs Finch's face had gone ice white. 'This . . . this is ridiculous,' she stuttered.

'Go on, Venus,' said Radcliff, with a nod.

Venus swallowed deeply.

'When Mrs Finch caught me out one night for being up after L.O.,' Venus began, 'she sent me to her study – to wait for her. When I came in here, I saw some box files on her desk. I'm a pretty nosey sort of person, so I decided to have a quick peek inside one of them. I know it was wrong, but my curiosity sometimes gets the better of me. I found some letters showing that Bertram's is experiencing some severe financial difficulties.'

'Is this true?' asked Radcliff, turning to face Mrs Finch. 'Because you told me just the other day that Bertram's is in – and I quote you – "an excellent financial situation".'

'It *is*,' replied Mrs Finch hastily. 'We just have . . . have . . . certain . . . cash-flow problems . . .'

'It's a bit more than that,' said Venus. 'The school is heavily in debt. It's fallen way behind with some of its payments to suppliers. I found a final warning letter from the bank about a sum of fifteen thousand pounds.'

Mrs Finch glared furiously at Venus. 'You had no right looking in those files,' she snapped.

'That's not the point, is it, Mrs Finch?' said Radcliff sharply. 'Whatever the rights and wrongs of looking in the files may be, Venus discovered that you've been *lying* about the school's financial position. I assume the files are up there?' Radcliff pointed to a long row of shelves, housing a large collection of files.

Mrs Finch went very red. 'Yes, that's them,' she replied testily.

'I'll need to take a good look at them,' Radcliff told her.

The headmistress seemed to rally herself. 'OK,' she huffed, 'so the school has some money worries and the bank sent me warning letters. That doesn't connect me in any way with the abduction. And besides, why would I get myself involved with a plot to kidnap two of *my own* students? Do you think I'm mad? The publicity for the school would be appalling. As you are all aware, I am completely dedicated to Bertram's and its good reputation. The idea of my being involved with a kidnap is preposterous and I resent it bitterly.'

She spat out this last word as if it was a venom.

'You didn't mean to get involved with a *kidnap* plot,' responded Venus.

Mrs Finch stared at her for a second, then turned to Radcliff. 'I thought you were implying that —'

'You got involved *unwittingly*,' went on Venus, before addressing the others. 'Because of the money situation, I had my suspicions about Mrs Finch. She desperately needed money but I was sure she'd never get involved in a kidnap plot. There was something that was niggling at me, something I just couldn't work out until ten minutes ago, as I was walking through the Great Hall.'

'What happened?' asked Tatiana.

'I stumbled on some silver flight cases left on the floor by the school photographer. That's when it hit me. I'd seen cases like that in the boot of the kidnappers' car. DCI Radcliff phoned one of her officers and he confirmed that some photographic equipment was found in their car.'

Venus paused for a second and then continued. 'Earlier in the week I chanced on the kidnappers. They were parked late at night on the drive leading to the back of the school. I heard them mention the word "negative" and saw the name Basildon Street on a map. Basildon Street is home to *The Daily Enquiry* newspaper. When I realised it was photographic stuff in the boot, it hit me that the word "negative" wasn't referring to something *bad*, as I'd initially thought; it was referring to a *photographic* negative. I asked the DCI if anything had happened recently at the offices of *The Daily Enquiry* and she told me that there'd been a break-in earlier this week. Guess what was stolen? Some cameras and a strip of *negatives* from one of this week's papers.'

'Where is all of this leading?' asked Mrs Finch edgily.

'Let her finish,' butted in Tatiana.

'This is what I think happened,' said Venus, looking at the headmistress. 'Harding and Smiler approached you saying they were photographers from *The Daily Enquiry*. They wanted to get some exclusive photos of the rising film starlet, Tatiana Fairfleet. They reckoned that you were the best way of getting to Tatiana. They said that if you leaked them the destination of one of the Founders' Week trips, they'd pay you a large sum of money.'

Miss Sutton stared at the headmistress, her mouth opening and closing in shock.

'To be sure they were genuine,' went on Venus, 'you demanded rock solid proof that they were who they said they were. So they broke into the offices of *The Daily Enquiry*, nicked some photographic gear and grabbed some negatives of *actual photos* that had been in this week's paper. When you saw these, you accepted that they were the real deal. So you told them about the museum trip and they handed you a large sum of cash. You thought you were just exposing Tatiana to a couple of paparazzi, when in reality you sold her out to a kidnap team.'

There was a staggered hush in the room. Venus could hear the low hum of the wind outside. It was at least a minute before anyone spoke again.

Mrs Finch opened her mouth to speak. 'First of all, there isn't a kernel of truth in anything Venus has just said,' the headmistress snarled. 'And besides, even if there was, she has absolutely no *proof*. A piece of paper showing that the school has some financial concerns doesn't exactly make me a hardened criminal. If I *had* received such a sum of money, then where is it now? You can check my bank account; you can check the school's bank account. I can assure you, there is no such payment in either of these places. And the reason for that is that I haven't committed any crime.' Mrs Finch finished her speech with grim determination in her voice.

'The money isn't in either of those places,' whispered Venus. 'But I think I know where it is.'

'Well, where is it, then?' asked Tatiana.

Venus looked round the circle. 'The night I saw Harding and Smiler on the drive, I was crossing the quad on my way back to my room when I saw Mrs Finch following me. I thought she was just on her L.O. prowl, but now I realise that she'd actually just been to *meet* Harding and Smiler – to hand over the museum info and to receive the cash. She spotted me – at least, she spotted *someone* over the other side of the quad. She knew she had to check out who it was, but she had a bag full of money on her. As I started to run away I heard a distant thudding sound. At the time I assumed it was Harding and Smiler's car backfiring. But it wasn't.

'On my first day here Mrs Finch showed me round. One of the things she pointed out was an old well at the far side of the quad. That was the noise I heard; it was a bag of money being thrown and hitting the bottom of the well. In the panic of the moment she flung it down there and I'm pretty sure she's left the money there, hoping that this whole thing will blow over.'

'But . . . but that well has not been used for over fifty years,' cried Mrs Finch defensively.

'So you won't mind us looking down there,' replied DCI Radcliff.

'I . . . I . . .' Mrs Finch was finally speechless.

'Off you go, DC Summers,' instructed Radcliff.

'Right away, ma'am,' Summers replied.

The seven minutes it took DC Summers to return felt

like several centuries to Venus. She could feel Mrs Finch's eyes boring into her skull the whole time.

Everyone turned round when DC Summers re-entered the office. In his right hand was a large brown holdall. Its zip was undone and a stash of fifty-pound notes gazed out.

Mrs Finch's face dropped.

For a second no one spoke.

'You'd have had a problem spending this money,' said DC Summers. 'They're all fakes.'

Radcliff stood up and walked over to Mrs Finch. 'Angela Finch,' began the DCI, 'I am arresting you for aiding and abetting a kidnapping. You have the right to remain silent. Anything you do say can and will be used against you in a court of law. Do you understand?'

A broken Mrs Finch nodded tearfully.

'Right,' announced DCI Radcliff. 'I've ordered a complete media blackout on this story and I'm determined that no details of this meeting be leaked.'

'What about the other girls?' asked Miss Sutton. 'They're dying to know if Venus and Tatiana are all right.'

'You can tell them that they witnessed a cash snatch in the museum shop and were both knocked down by the thieves,' explained Radcliff. 'That is the official story. They were taken to hospital suffering from mild shock and arrived back at Bertram's in the early hours of this morning.'

'I'm not sure they'll buy that,' replied Miss Sutton.

'They'll have no choice,' responded Radcliff, 'because that will be the only story in town. As for Mrs Finch – she was called away on family business in the middle of the night. Do you all understand this?

Everyone nodded.

'Right,' continued Radcliff, 'I want the rest of you to go and get some sleep. Mrs Finch, I'd like you to come with me and DC Summers.'

Venus, Tatiana and Miss Sutton shuffled out of the room. Just before she got to the door, Venus took a quick glance back. Mrs Finch's face appeared to have crumpled in on itself and her hands were shaking.

Venus found herself feeling a bit sorry for the distraught headmistress.

Venus slept until well into the afternoon. When she finally managed to get out of bed, she found a note under her door.

Miss Sutton told us we couldn't disturb you, but we're desperate to see you. What happened to you and Tatiana? Where have you been?
Come and find us the second you're up.
Jaz + Geri

Venus opened her bedroom door. Acc Block 2 was very quiet. Of course! It was Saturday and it was a sunny afternoon. All of the girls would probably be outside, enjoying a lesson-free day.

Venus got dressed and hurried off to find Tatiana. She knocked once on her door and called, 'It's me.'

The door was opened almost instantly. Tatiana stood there, looking exhausted.

'I'm so glad you came,' said Tatiana, smiling. 'We need to go over our story, don't we?'

'That's exactly why I'm here.' Venus grinned back.

'Come in,' said Tatiana. 'I was just breaking open a packet of KitKats.'

It took Venus and Tatiana an hour to get their story straight, twenty minutes to locate Jaz and Geri (they were way out on the Sculpted Lawns) and another hour to tell them everything. Daisy and Zaynab came in for the last part and Venus had to recap some of it for their benefit.

'How are you both feeling now?' asked Jaz, still reeling from shock at their story and amazed that Tatiana was not only speaking to them, but was also being really friendly! What had Venus done to her? Given her a complete personality makeover?

'We're OK,' answered Venus. 'The whole thing seemed so unreal at the time, but now it feels like it really happened. Thank God we were *both* there when the thieves struck. I would hate to have gone through that by myself.'

'Me too,' said Tatiana, nodding earnestly.

'Which hospital did you go to?' asked Daisy.

Tatiana opened her mouth but kept silent, her cheeks starting to redden.

'Er . . . Fordham General,' replied Venus hastily.

Luckily she'd seen a sign to it on the coach journey to the museum.

'And what's happened to old Finchy?' asked Jaz. 'Miss

Sutton said she had to rush off last night – family problems or something.'

'Yeah,' added Geri. 'And it all seems pretty serious. The way Miss Sutton was talking it sounded like Finchy might not be coming back.'

Venus and Tatiana quickly glanced at each other but said nothing.

After supper, Venus showed Tatiana her spot on the roof. They sat looking out over the rapidly darkening countryside.

'It was brave of you to go and check out their car that night,' said Tatiana.

'Brave – or stupid?' asked Venus.

'Brave,' replied Tatiana. 'If you hadn't gone out there and heard what you did, Mrs Finch might have got away with it.' She paused. 'I still can't believe she'd sell me out to the press.'

'People who are desperate for money do stupid things,' said Venus. 'The tabloid thing probably seemed like a quick, easy way to get money. No one would get hurt. The only downside as far as she was concerned was that you'd get your pictures in the papers – but that's not exactly unusual for a rising movie star. Harding and Smiler, or whatever their names really are, must have been totally convincing.'

They were silent for a few seconds.

'So what happens next for you?' asked Tatiana.

Venus shrugged her shoulders. 'I'll go back to school and hang out with Kate. I'm spending most of half-term with Dennis on the set of *Velocity Sparks* at Elstree. It's got Saffron Ritchie in it, so I'll check out for signs of the boob job.'

Tatiana laughed.

'Anyway,' said Venus, 'what about you? You've got *Flash Point Nine* coming up, haven't you?'

Tatiana nodded. 'Yeah. It's three weeks' filming in southern Spain.'

'You poor thing,' said Venus. 'Three weeks off school, spent catching rays. It's a tough life, being an actress.'

Tatiana laughed. 'I can assure you I'll be working pretty hard and besides, the temperature is crazy over there at the moment.'

'I'm gutted for you,' said Venus with a smile.

'Look,' said Tatiana, suddenly sounding all serious. 'I'm really sorry about everything. You put yourself in danger because of me and I acted like a complete prima donna and . . .'

'I've told you already, forget it,' answered Venus. 'It's over. You've already apologised about a zillion times.'

'OK, OK,' said Tatiana. 'I just wanted you to know that I can be OK.'

'It's cool,' said Venus. 'You did great back there when it came down to it.'

Tatiana smiled gratefully for this approval.

* * *

The minute Venus went back inside room 219, her mobile went off.

'Venus, it's Radcliff.'

'Oh, hi.'

'Just to let you know that Mrs Finch has formally resigned as headmistress of Bertram's, with immediate effect. She's only two years away from retirement anyway. She's highly traumatised by her role in this affair and she'll be facing criminal charges. They'll go a bit lenient on her because of her age, previous good character and the fact she was unaware of the kidnap plot.'

'Will she go to prison?'

'Unlikely. I think she'll suffer enough without being locked up.' She paused and then continued. 'You know what I said about no heroics, Venus?'

Uh oh, I sense another lecture.

'Yeah?'

'I still stand by that,' said Radcliff, 'but I have to say you did really well out there.'

'Thanks.'

'However, just because you managed to escape from them, doesn't mean you can go round thinking you're Wonder Woman.'

'I'll leave that role up to you,' said Venus, laughing.

Radcliff said nothing, but Venus could almost hear her smile down the line.

'OK,' said Radcliff, 'go home tomorrow and get on with the rest of your life. We may not meet again, but you never know – our paths may cross.'

'Let's see,' said Venus.

The phone call ended.

Venus lay on her bed for a while, going back over the

events of the last few days that were still spinning in her head. In a way she'd be more than happy if she never set eyes on Radcliff again. Wherever the DCI was, trouble seemed to follow. But on the other hand, just like after stunt camp, Venus felt a shiny glow of elation surrounding her. She'd got Tatiana and herself out of an amazingly dangerous situation. And she'd relied on her stunt skills to do it. Wasn't that saying something? Wasn't that a massive achievement?

It was only then that she realised how completely exhausted she was. She needed sleep – and lots of it.

SUNDAY

Venus packed after breakfast and took her stuff down to the Great Hall.

She'd said goodbye to Daisy and Zaynab in the Refectory.

Jaz and Geri walked with her to the Great Hall.

'We're gonna miss you,' said Jaz.

'I can't believe it's only been a week,' said Geri, smiling. 'It feels like a year.'

'So true.' Venus grinned. 'Maybe even *two* years.'

They all laughed.

'Are you OK after the thieves and everything?' asked Jaz.

'Yeah – we were so worried,' said Geri.

'I can't believe you had to go to hospital to be treated for shock,' added Jaz.

'There are far worse things that could have happened,' said Venus bravely.

'What's happened to Tatiana Fairfleet?' Jaz asked. 'She's treating us like humans and not bits of dirt scraped off the bottom of her Hollywood boots.'

Venus laughed. 'Shock can do that to people – especially actress types. She's actually really nice.' Changing the subject, Venus said, 'Good luck with your new headmistress.'

'Thanks,' said Jaz. 'It will be *so* weird without Finchy.'

'Weird – or fantastic?' asked Geri.

'The next head may be worse,' pointed out Jaz.

'Impossible!' replied Geri.

'You will keep in touch, won't you?' asked Jaz. 'Let us know what happens with Jed and everything.'

Venus blushed slightly. 'Of course I will,' she said. 'And you guys keep me posted with all of your boyfriend news and any dramas here.'

'You bet,' said Jaz, grinning.

Both girls gave Venus massive hugs and then let her go. They went back in the direction of the quad and Venus went in the other direction, towards the front of the school.

She stepped out of the main door on to the now familiar drive where Tatiana and Miss Sutton were waiting for her. There was a taxi parked there too, driven by a woman with short bleached hair and rosy cheeks.

'I guess this is it,' said Venus.

Miss Sutton fixed Venus with an earnest gaze. 'Mrs Finch did a terrible thing, and I'm so sorry you got caught up in it. I keep on telling myself that she really believed she was doing it in the best interests of the school.'

Venus smiled. That was such a Miss Sutton thing to say – she was a really positive person.

'Anyway,' added her form tutor, brightening up. 'It's been a pleasure having you in my tutor group – you've certainly made things livelier in Founders' Week! In fact, we've never had a week anything like this!'

Venus laughed.

Miss Sutton smiled at her. 'You take care of yourself,' she added. 'You're an amazingly gifted – not to mention, extremely brave – girl. I would hate for anything bad to ever happen to you.'

'Sure,' replied Venus. 'I'll stay out of trouble.'

Miss Sutton shook Venus's hand and then went back into the school.

Tatiana then stepped forward and hugged Venus so tightly she almost needed an oxygen mask.

'Thank you, thank you, thank you,' said the beaming actress, finally releasing Venus from her grasp. 'I owe you big time.'

'Nah,' replied Venus. 'You don't owe me. But just make sure that if Dennis doesn't get tickets for the *Airborne Sword* première, you'll get one for me.'

Tatiana bowed dramatically. 'Consider it done,' she replied.

'Cheers,' Venus said.

'Oh and Venus,' added Tatiana, 'sorry for being so . . .'

'Enough!' Venus grinned. 'It's all in the past.'

'Good,' said Tatiana, smiling.

Venus climbed into the back of the cab and lowered the window. 'I'll come back and visit someday,' she said.

'You better,' said Tatiana.

Venus laughed. 'And in a couple of years, when you need a body double in a film, remember who to ask for!'

Tatiana pulled a face of comedic uncertainty. 'Now who could that be?' she mused.

They were suddenly silent.

'OK,' Venus said eventually. 'I guess it's goodbye.'

'I guess it is. Thanks for everything Venus.'

Venus grinned and the cab pulled away and headed off down the drive.

Tatiana stood there waving.

The cab reached the end of the drive and turned left. Venus closed the window and prepared for the return to her 'real' world. Being a kidnap escapee might have been a white-knuckle, adrenaline-pumped experience, but there was no way she could do it on a daily basis.

Back at home, Venus's mum plied her with questions.

'Was it a good experience? Would you do it again? What kind of things were better than at your school?'

After fifteen minutes of grilling, Venus held up her hand. 'Interrogation over!' she declared.

Gail laughed. 'Sorry, I'm just fascinated by the whole thing. When I was a kid I sometimes dreamed of going to one of those really ancient boarding schools – I thought it would be my passport to success in the adult world.'

'You haven't done too badly without it,' replied Venus.

Gail smiled. 'Thanks. I'm not moaning about a terrible childhood – Dad and Mum were great parents – I just used to think about those kinds of schools.'

'Bertram's is in a different dimension, Mum. You should see the Sculpted Lawns. They go on for ever. You can walk for miles and still be on land that's owned by the school.'

Gail nodded. 'A lot of these establishments have been

around for hundreds of years. It's amazing that they've all lasted for so long.'

'The best thing was that the girls weren't really like I thought they would be,' said Venus. 'Sure there were a few princesses in there, but most of them seemed like me and my mates. You know, they're into music, hanging out . . .'

'And boys?' asked Gail.

'Stop it, Mum,' protested Venus, 'you're embarrassing me.'

'Sorry,' said Gail, smiling. 'Did you speak to Jed when you were there?'

Venus pulled a face. 'Yeah. You know the weekend he was going to come down?'

'The one he was going to spend with his uncle in London?'

'Yeah. He's not coming.'

An hour later Venus was all talked out. As soon as Gail had finished her questioning, Kate appeared and Venus told her everything. Her jaw ached by the end of this, but it was such a relief to tell someone the truth about her crazy week at Bertram's.

Kate looked at Venus with amazement. 'What is it with you, Venus? You nearly got yourself killed at stunt camp and now here you are risking it all again. Do you have a death wish or something?'

Venus laughed. 'Nah. If Tatiana hadn't left that auditorium I'm not sure any of it would have happened.'

'The plain-clothes officers sounded like they were

asleep, so it probably *would* have,' replied Kate.

'Well, anyway, it's all over, and I promise you there'll be no more mad excitement for me in the immediate future. I have school and homework and assignments to look forward to . . .' Venus's voice trailed off.

'I know,' said Kate, grinning. 'I've only been back a week and my work is piling up.'

Half an hour after Kate had left, the landline rang. Venus picked it up. It was Dennis.

'Can you pop over?' he asked.

'Sure. Tomorrow night?'

'Could you come now?'

Venus checked her watch. 'OK. I'll leave in five minutes.'

'Great.'

She paused. Dennis's voice sounded a bit weird – a bit strained.

'Are you OK, Granddad?'

He coughed. 'I'm fine. Why?'

'Nothing. I'll see you in a bit.'

'Good.'

Gail walked into the room as Venus replaced the handset.

'Who was that?' Gail asked.

Venus looked round. 'It was Granddad. I'm just popping over to see him.'

Gail frowned. 'OK,' she said, 'but don't stay there for hours. You're back at school tomorrow, remember?'

How could I forget.

She grabbed her bike and wheeled it outside.

She was about to climb on, when her mobile went. JED, said the screen.

She answered it immediately.

'Hey, Venus, you're not going to believe this.'

What? More bad news?

'My Australian uncle broke his leg playing tennis. He's fine, but it means that they've cancelled their trip.'

Poor uncle but YESSSSSSSSSSS!

'So our weekend's back on?'

'Completely! Gotta go. Speak to you soon!'

Venus pedalled like mad. Jed would come down to London as they'd originally planned. Superb! Brilliant! Fantastic!

Her thoughts turned to Dennis. She reckoned she'd worked out why he'd sounded a bit funny; he must have got those tickets for the *Airborne Sword* première. He probably just wanted to tell her face to face. That was one of the great things about Dennis: he was always true to his word. She pedalled faster. The première was going to be a truly excellent occasion. By the time she arrived at Dennis's she was still wondering what she would wear for the big night. It was a major film première after all – it had to be worth making a bit of an effort.

Dennis opened the door before she'd had a chance to ring the bell.

'Come in,' he said quietly.

Venus wheeled her bike inside and propped it against the wall. Dennis stood in the hallway.

'Have you got them?' Venus asked breathlessly.

'Got what?' he asked with uncertainty.

'The *Airborne Sword* tickets – the ones you promised me? That's what this is all about, isn't it? That's why you sounded a bit strange on the phone.'

'Sorry, Venus,' he replied softly, 'I haven't had a chance to get those yet. But I'm on the case. We will go.'

Venus pulled a puzzled expression. 'Is it about Kelly Tanner, then? Am I going to meet her?'

Dennis shook his head. His expression had suddenly turned very, very serious. Venus took a step back. She'd seen him lose his temper plenty of times, but she wasn't sure this was a bad-temper kind of serious look. This was something quite different. He seemed totally on edge, as if he was about to announce that someone had died while she'd been away. His eyes kept flickering in the direction of the kitchen.

'What's going on?' she demanded, her eyes moving from the kitchen back to him.

Dennis took a very deep breath.

Suddenly Venus became aware of another presence in the house. A shadow from the kitchen was thrown across the hallway carpet.

'Who's there?' Venus asked.

A man walked out of the kitchen into the hallway.

He was tall and wiry, with blue eyes and short, sandy hair. He was wearing a crumpled white linen suit. He walked over and stopped a couple of metres short of them.

'Hello, Venus,' he said in an American accent. 'I'm Elliot Nevis. I'm your dad.'